Chamomile Flower
Flowers of Evil

Robert V. Wadden Jr.

Chapter One
New York City

The crowd at the Red Room at DL, a club on the lower East Side, trended young, well dressed and Caucasian. Techno pop boomed out over a crowded dance floor lit by blinking red spotlights. The bar was busy and the vibe was intense. Brandon Dorsey could almost smell the animal pheromones emanating from the crowd as he picked his way around the dance floor.

At thirty-two Brandon was the second son of a family that had been wealthy for four generations starting with food processing plants in Brooklyn leading to a present-day Manhattan real estate empire and impressive stock portfolio. Nominally Brandon was a vice president of Dorsey Enterprises, the family holding company. This involved him showing up at his office in the Dorsey Building one or two days a week for a few hours. Older brother Merritt ran the company so Brandon's duties were non-existent. His salary and monthly distributions from the family trust fund afforded him a lavish lifestyle with ample time to enjoy it. Leisure time and money left him bored and depressed. It seemed that lately only a plethora of antidepressants kept him afloat. His visit to DL was to find female companionship for the night. Brandon's active and diverse love life left him deeply unsatisfied. He seemed always to be looking for something he did not understand and could not find.

As he approached the busy bar staffed by female bar tenders hustling to fill drink orders, he spotted a woman with long, silky, jet-black hair leaning against the bar. She was dressed in a stylish blue silk sleeveless dress hemmed just above the knees. She wore matching patent leather stiletto heels at the end of a pair of toned, elegant, shapely legs. As he approached, she turned toward him and he saw that her face was lovely; pale skin, sculpted cheekbones, huge blue eyes. Around her neck was a silver chain with a large pale blue sapphire. She seemed to be looking right at him even though he was fifteen feet away.

As smoothly as he could he sidled up next to her at the bar. "Can I buy you a drink?" he asked hoping his extreme nervousness was not apparent.

"Of course," she answered looking directly at him.

Her smile seemed somehow without joy and something about it sent a chill down his spine.

"I'm Brandon," he said nodding at her.

"Ariella," she answered with that same mirthless smile. "I've just come into town on business. I've never been here before. Is it always this chaotic?"

"Almost always. Sundays are the only quiet nights. Does all the noise and activity bother you?"

"Yes, I'm a solitary person most of the time but occasionally I get the urge to roam a bit. What about you?"

"Restless. I always seem to be looking for something, if that makes any sense."

"It makes perfect sense. I think I know exactly what you mean and what you are looking for."

"Really? Because I don't. You said you were in town on business. What do you do?"

"Consulting," she said almost wearily as if she were tired of talking about it. "I'm done for this trip so it's time to have some fun."

"What do you consider fun?"

"Maybe you'd like to find out. I have a feeling we share the same definition."

"What would that entail?" he asked, his interest aroused.

"It would entail you being open to possibilities. It would entail you meeting me at the Zephyr Hotel on Bergen Street and booking a room."

"Isn't that in Spanish Harlem? That's a dangerous neighborhood, especially for two people dressed like we are."

"Suit yourself," she said and turned away.

"Let's have that drink I offered and I'll meet you there."

"Great, Brandon. Look, we need to take separate cars just to keep things discreet. You go first, book the room and I'll meet you in the lobby. I guarantee you won't be disappointed."

"I'll hold you to that guarantee," said Brandon smiling.

Chapter Two
New York City

Lydia Garber rambled on about her marital problems. Her husband was insensitive, he only cared about money, she was sure he was being unfaithful, he had erectile dysfunction, was uncaring and rude. Doctor Elise Bloom was struggling to appear alert and intense despite being thoroughly bored by her patient's complaints. When Mrs. Garber paused to take a breath, Elise managed to comment. "Have you raised any of these issues with your husband? How does he respond?"

"Well, he doesn't. I mean, no, I haven't actually broached any of these issues directly to him, but I'm sure he must know how I feel."

"Mrs. Garber, I'm a clinical therapist. What you need is a marriage counselor. I am not hearing anything to indicate that you have serious mental or emotional issues, just that you are unsatisfied with your marriage. I'm going to recommend that you try to get your husband to accompany you into couples' therapy. I can recommend an excellent therapist who specializes in counseling couples. I think that is the right course for you."

After further discussion a frustrated Lydia Garber left the office none too pleased with her therapist. Elise doubted she would take her advice about marriage counseling and she suspected the husband would be uncooperative. Elise had a full schedule of clients, most of whom had much more serious problems than Mrs. Garber, as well as a contract with the Federal Bureau of Prisons to provide inmate counseling and evaluation two days a week at the Metropolitan Correctional Center in Manhattan. She could well afford to lose a patient who did not need her services.

At thirty Elise built a successful career as a clinical therapist. With an undergraduate degree from Yale and her doctorate from Harvard her credentials were stellar. Her reputation as a skilled, ethical therapist was beyond reproach. She maintained an elegant and expensive office on Manhattan's West side. Her personal life was considerably less satisfying. She was married for two years to a bond broker, a partner at Goldman Sachs. In retrospect those were the worst two years of her life. Her ex-husband was arrogant, emotionally abusive, and distant. She married him because he was exceedingly handsome. She was attracted to his success and confidence. However, it turned out they had almost nothing in common. He cared only about money and status with no intellectual curiosity. Elise was always immersed in a book or reading scholarly psychology papers. She loved music both jazz and classical. He never read for pleasure and was indifferent to music of any kind. His primary, if not sole, interest in life was in making money. The divorce was predictably acrimonious and for the last few years she had been without a partner. Internet dating apps resulted in utter failure at best and the occasional disaster at worst.

Finding someone compatible with an intellectually oriented, introverted, clinical psychologist was not an easy match. Her friends told her she was quite beautiful. She had clear, pale skin, large green eyes, long blonde hair that fell in curly ringlets to her shoulders and an attractive figure. She always made every effort to dim whatever attractiveness she had, feeling it was a professional disadvantage. In graduate school, surrounded by mostly male colleagues, she had a hard time being taken seriously. There seemed to be a prevailing mythology that pretty girls could not be smart. So, she wore her hair back in a pony-tail, wore wire rimmed glasses instead of contacts and little or no makeup. She dressed in baggy, drab colored clothes to hide her figure and blend into the background. She wanted her patients to take her seriously as a professional and she did not want to distract the prisoners she interviewed for the Bureau of Prisons.

She should have been happy. She had the career she always wanted, the work was fulfilling and interesting. She was good at it. If her parents were still alive, they would have been exceedingly proud of their only child. Something was missing from her life and she was beginning to feel as if she were simply trudging through life with no goal or direction and little meaning.

Chapter Three
Zephyr Hotel, New York City

The crime scene was grisly. The Zephyr was a cheap hotel in Spanish Harlem. The building was close to one hundred years old and looked as if it had not ever been renovated. There was dust on the surface of the plywood dresser, the carpet was worn and stained as were the walls. The corpse on the bed had its eyes open, its face frozen with a look of terror. His neck was mottled with purple bruises and his face was bruised, gray, drained of blood. "Looks like he was strangled, I'm guessing by hand. There are no ligature marks from a cord or line," said Detective Ermina Gonzales to her boss.

"I'm not seeing much sign of a struggle. It looks like the poor guy had an orgasm before or during his demise," responded Detective Becky Haden who oversaw the investigation.

"We need to see if we can get any DNA samples from the bed or his body. Go question the night clerk as to who checked in and who he might have been with," she directed a uniformed officer standing by the door.

"Do we have any idea who this guy is?" she asked Gonzales.

"His ID says he is Brandon Dorsey. There's a drivers' license, credit cards and a little over a thousand dollars in cash. I think we can rule out robbery as a motive here."

"I'm thinking crime of passion," replied Haden.

"What, do people really choke each other when they have sex, is that a thing?"

Haden smiled. Sometimes Gonzalez, for all her tough girl from the hood swagger, could seem naïve.

"Yeah, it can be a thing between consenting adults. I don't think our Mister Dorsey consented to this." Gonzales chuckled.

She liked Haden and was grateful to be assigned to another

woman as her first partner in Homicide. Haden was smart and tough. She was patient and tried to teach Gonzales, not just order her around. As one of the first women in the division Haden had to prove herself the way no man had been required. She was even involved with the FBI in a case which resulted in two agents being murdered, one right in front of Haden. At least that was the story about her that circulated Homicide. Supposedly she had gotten the woman responsible for killing both agents, shot in a marina in Costa Rica. Haden would not discuss the case.

The uniform officer came back from the lobby. "Detective Haden, the night clerk said this guy checked in about two A.M., he hung around in the lobby after getting his key waiting for someone. After about twenty minutes a woman showed up and they went to his room."

"Did you get a description of the woman?" asked Haden.

"Yeah, late twenties, Caucasian, very light skinned, long dark hair, blue dress, blue eyes, silver chain with a blue stone around her neck."

"What?" said Haden.

"Yeah, the clerk remembered her because he said she was hot, I mean, you know attractive. That's why the description is so good."

"You think the woman was the perp, boss?" asked Gonzales.

"Yeah, I just hope it's not who I think it might be. It can't be, it shouldn't be but I guess it could."

"Boss, you know who did it?"

"I don't know but let's have the night clerk come into the office and we will show him some photos. That might help."

The morgue guys came to pick up the body. They went back to their offices to finish the paperwork on the incident while the crime scene team dusted for fingerprints and took DNA samples. Gonzales came into Haden's cubicle with a print-out. "This Dorsey guy was a big shot from a very wealthy family," she said.

"Well, we kind of guessed that from his clothes. Custom made suit, hand tailored linen shirt. His shoes were easily worth six hundred new. Anything from the morgue yet?"

"Yeah, they got fingerprints from around Dorsey's neck, he was strangled to death by someone's bare hands like we suspected. They ran the prints and couldn't come up with a match. They did get some DNA samples from Dorsey's body but it takes a while to run them. The coroner's report will take a couple of days but there is no mystery how he died."

"Okay. We need to check Uber, Lyft, and taxis to see who dropped these two off at the Zephyr and where they came from. Get people on that right away. Is that night clerk here yet?"

"Yeah, boss, he's waiting in interrogation room twelve."

Haden reached into her desk pulling out a manila folder.

"Stop calling me boss. We've worked together long enough you can call me Becky, or even Haden if you prefer."

She got up and Gonzales followed her to the interrogation room. Haden selected three stock photos from files on the way there.

The clerk was sitting by himself looking nervous. "Sorry to drag you here," said Haden. "We need to see if you can give us a more positive ID of the woman who showed up last night with the victim."

She spread the three stock photos on the table in front of him. Each was of a dark-haired woman in her late twenties or early thirties. She slipped a photograph out of her manila folder and placed it next to the stock photos. It too was of a dark-haired woman in the same age range.

"That's her for sure. Yeah, that's the woman. Still fresh in my mind. She was hot man. Not many chicks like that show up at the Zephyr."

The picture he was pointing to was the one Haden pulled out of her manila folder.

Chapter Four
Villa Dupleve, Guadeloupe, French Caribbean

The water was intensely blue with sunlight glinting on the surface in flecks of gold. The waves were flat, quietly lapping the shore with a rhythmic sound. A faint floral smell from the villa's gardens filled the air. In the banana groves adjacent to the villa the broad leaves of the banana trees fluttered like butterfly wings while branches loaded with fruit and strange conical flowers bobbed. Ariella lay nude on her chaise lounge on her private beach. On a small metal table next to her was an ice bucket with a bottle of champagne and a half-filled glass. As it always did the ocean and the warm sun calmed her.

She completely lost her cool with that Brandon guy. She left behind evidence she never would have in a professional hit. She was not sure what got into her. She could have beaten him without killing him. She knew when to stop. She had done it with other boyfriends. This time she just could not stop. When she knew he was dead she did not even bother to clean up. She just grabbed her purse and left out the service entrance. The night clerk saw her as had people at the club when she was leaving with the guy. A good cop could track down the taxi that dropped her off at the hotel Zephyr.

She wondered, not for the first time, if it was time to stop killing. Could she stop killing? Money was no longer the motivation. She was rich. She had a robust stock portfolio, real estate holdings in Los Angeles that generated significant rent. She paid no taxes on her primary income. The proceeds of her assassinations were paid into offshore banks without a hint to the Internal Revenue Service. Her investments were held by multiple Panamanian holding companies with proceeds going into Panamanian bank accounts. Ariella Blumkin, the individual, did not exist, had not existed since she graduated from college. The problem with not killing was her hunger for prey.

Long ago her mother called her a "monster." Her first real lover, a Russian literature professor at UCLA, echoed that accusation before dumping her. While both suffered the consequences of failing her, she ultimately had to accept they were right. She was a monster. She accepted that and felt no worse about it than she did any one of the many killings she committed. Guilt, regret, shame, sorrow none of these emotions made any sense to her because she never experienced them. She realized that made her different than most people and it made her hard for people to understand.

Her housekeeper, Amelie came down the stairs from the villa to the beach with a tray of charcuterie and a fresh bottle of champagne. Amelie was no longer uncomfortable at seeing her employer nude on the private beach. Since Ariella paid her a handsome salary, flew her mother to Paris for surgery and put them up in a hotel while she recovered, Amelie felt fierce loyalty to this strange woman.

Ariella looked up at her and smiled. Amelie had gotten very good at anticipating Ariella's wants and needs without being asked. Life here on the island was good. The sun was hot, the ocean was warm, there was good French food and wine, fresh seafood, and the serenity of the privacy of her villa. Ariella could see someday permanently retreating to this place, abandoning her deadly career, especially if she could find someone with whom to share it. Monsters needed love too.

Chapter Five
Saint Petersburg, Russia

Even in the spring the city could be chilly. Arkady Boromir strolled down the cobblestone street in the old town. What had once been a nineteenth century noble family's palace was now an office building housing, among other enterprises, two floors leased by Pantera, JSC, known in the Western media as "Evil Corp." It was a wholly owned subsidiary of Arkin, JSC which in turn was owned by a consortium of Russian banks and fossil fuel companies. Arkin had contracts with the Russian government which allowed it to infuse cash into Pantera. Of course, lately Pantera was bringing in substantial revenues on its own.

Arkady was a computer analyst who specialized in hacking complex computer service systems to impose ransomware. The most recent Pantera project had stopped the flow of an oil pipeline on the east coast of the United States. The project was successful causing chaos in several American cities with long lines for gasoline and transit services suspended. The current American administration was savagely criticized by its political rivals for allowing it to happen. While ultimately American technicians figured a way around the hack after several days and no ransom was paid, Arkady's employers were very happy with the efforts of their team.

Arkady entered the lobby of the venerable building checking in with security and scanning a badge which allowed him access to an elevator going to the fifth and sixth floors. The fifth floor was a maze of cubicles separated by four-foot partitions. Each cubicle had a small metal desk and two or three large monitors along with a keyboard and mouse set-up. Arkady's cubicle had a small picture of his fiancé and a vase of fresh chamomile flowers, the national flower of mother Russia.

Upstairs on the sixth floor were banks of computer servers connected by cable to the various node computers in the individual cubicles. Pantera had over one hundred and thirty employees and hundreds of millions of rubles worth of hardware on the two floors of the old Vordinsky palace.

Arkady grabbed a mug of tea from the samovar in the break room and sat down at his computer. He and several colleagues were working on inserting a virus into the operating system of a large New York City hospital. A series of e-mails with the embedded virus would be sent to various hospital employees. Any employee opening the e-mail would enable the virus to infect the operating system rendering the hospital's computer system inert. Subsystems like climate control, security, diagnostic systems, oxygen control, electrical distribution and sanitation systems would be frozen as well as all computer communication functions. Because hospitals dealt in life-or-death situations, they were most vulnerable to this type of hacking and most likely to pay promptly to restore systems. Right now, Arkady and his compatriots were working to design ways for the virus to defeat the hospital's sophisticated security protocols. This was just a matter of time.

Future projects would include a plan to interfere with delivery of electricity and natural gas to utility consumers. Shutting down large sectors of the American electrical grid would have major political repercussions. Already the American ambassador was begging the Kremlin to put pressure on hackers. The Americans knew full well that these activities were subsidized and encouraged by the Russian government. The Kremlin was officially in full denial that any such activities could possibly be occurring in Russia.

Chapter Six
New York City, NYPD Headquarters, One Police Plaza

Haden reviewed the reports from the Dorsey investigation that had just been delivered. Dorsey called an Uber to a club on the lower east side at about one ten AM. He gave specific instructions to take him to the Zephyr hotel. He was dropped off about twenty-five minutes later in front of the hotel. Neither the club nor the hotel had security cameras. A taxi company reported one of their cabs picking up a young woman at the same club fifteen minutes after Dorsey left. The cab dropped her off at the Zephyr a little before two AM. She paid in cash. The cabbie was brought in and identified the woman from a photo provided by Haden.

"Who is this woman?" asked Gonzales. "How the hell did you know to pull out that photo to get the ID?"

"It's a long story," sighed Haden "but when I heard the description the night clerk at the Zephyr gave, I had a pretty strong hunch it was someone I knew."

"So, is this some dominatrix who gets her rocks off by having kinky sex?"

"She's a lot more than that. She's a professional killer who left a lot of bodies in her wake. What confuses me is that the Dorsey killing is not like her at all. She normally kills for money but as far as we can tell no one wanted Dorsey dead and no one was likely to foot the bill for an expensive assassin. She never left fingerprints at a crime scene before or DNA samples. There was no clean-up. This had the feel of a spur of the moment killing. Maybe one where she lost control. Her past crimes seemed to show a killer who was very much in control."

"Are you sure it's her?"

"The IDs are strong but our girl had a California driver's license under the name Amy Zyler. If we check the California DMV data base, we should get a match."

Haden forwarded the request to forensics and within a half hour got back a confirmation. The fingerprints found on Dorsey's neck were a match for those on record for Amy Zyler. Haden picked up the phone and dialed FBI Assistant director Patricia Patterson in Washington D.C.

"Hello detective," answered Patterson "to what do I owe the honor of this phone call? Have you changed your mind and decided to apply to come work for the Bureau?"

"No, sorry, it's not about that. I'm afraid I have some bad news for you. Our girl, the one who shot agents Diaz and VanDerlies is alive. We just linked her to a killing here in New York. We have a positive witness ID and fingerprints." There was a brief silence on the other end of the line.

"You told me after VanDerlies was killed that the blood they found on the boat where we thought she had been shot did not match the birth record for Ariella Blumkin. I have to admit at the time I didn't believe you. I thought there had to be a mistake, a mix-up of some sort. I guess I just wanted to believe it was ended. So, if she committed this murder, do you have any way to locate her to make an arrest?"

"We tried to track her movements after she left the crime scene but we couldn't pick up anything. There are not a lot of surveillance cameras in that part of Manhattan. We couldn't find a taxi or any other means for her to leave the area so we are at a loss for her whereabouts."

"You put out a notice to airports, bus stations, car rentals with her description?"

"Yes ma'am. So far, no response. You know the woman uses disguises. We have to assume she has a fake passport of some kind. It's possible by now she is out of the country."

"Looks like it's time to go on the hunt again. I hesitate to assign an agent since every-one who has gone after her so far is dead. I have an idea who might be the right person for this. Haden, we are once again going to need your help. We have to get her this time. I don't want to lose any more agents. I'll contact your boss and get clearance for you to work on this for us."

"I have some ideas about how we might get her in our sights again. Have your agent contact me and we'll get to work on it." Haden hung up and looked up at Gonzales. "Looks like we have FBI help on this one."

"I don't see how you expect to locate her. We may have a case with decent evidence but we have no perp," said Gonzales.

"My little escapade in Costa Rica taught us a few things about our girl that may help us. Maybe VanDerlies didn't die in vain after all."

Chapter Seven
Bogota, Colombia

Even in summer the air in Bogota could be clear and crisp, at least if you stayed out of the worst parts of town. Arturo Escalante, number one in the Cadrio faction of the Medellin cartel was in town to meet with the other four members of the governing directorate of the cartel. Each member represented a separate faction which had all been independent cartels in the days following the break-up of the original Pablo Escobar cartel and the fall of the powerful Cali cartel. After a period of bloodshed, the Medellin cartels came together to form a federation that would work together to manufacture and market cocaine for the U.S. and European markets. The federation had been a great success. Now that they were working together, the bloodshed ceased and their production and sales boomed. There was plenty of *dinero* for everyone and the peace allowed them to enjoy the fruits of their labors without fear of being gunned down or blown up.

Instrumental in their success had been the efforts of their lawyer Carlos Bonilla. It was Bonilla who used his connections to find a highly skilled assassin to kill the leaders of rival cartel *Los Urbenos* which had been competing with Medellin for the U.S. market. Escobar disliked Bonilla but had to admit he was seldom wrong and steered the cartel to make some good decisions. Bonilla was not one of them. He was not born in Medellin, grew up rich and well connected, educated in the best schools. He hobnobbed with members of the national legislature and the wealthiest most influential businessmen. Technically Bonilla was not a member of the cartel nor its governing board. He had no vote. He was the cartel's lawyer, did not participate in their profits but was paid generously for his services. Indeed, Bonilla did not appear to have any other clients.

Escalante accepted that a smart, well-connected lawyer was an asset to the cartel. He admitted that Bonilla had steered them in the right direction and guided them to some good and profitable decisions. The problem Escalante had with Bonilla was that increasingly he was acting as the de facto leader of the cartel. He started suggesting policies and actions to the governing board. They usually followed his lead. Increasingly whenever a decision had to be made the board looked to him to suggest a course of action. He had become far more than just a lawyer and Escalante was determined to do something about it.

The subject of this day's meeting was the fate of Alfonso Morales. He was a major distributor of cocaine in New York City. The cartel recently obtained information that Morales was skimming profits due the cartel. His own agreed upon share had been unduly generous in Escalante's opinion but for Morales to fake sales figures in order to claim more was intolerable. There was a need to bring this hog to slaughter.

The meeting was being held in a suite at the Four Seasons Casa Medina hotel. Escalante arrived just as a white jacketed waiter was serving drinks to Roberto Alfaro and Juan Solis, two of the other board members. Escalante took a tumbler of twenty-three-year-old Bunnahbhain single malt whiskey. Tasso Almonte and David Zaragosa, the two other members of the cartel board, arrived and got their drinks. "Shall we get started," asked Escalante.

"Bonilla is not here yet, let's wait," said Almonte.

"Look, since Bonilla is not here yet can we discuss him for a moment?" said Escalante. "Bonilla was a good counselor to us at first but he is becoming something more now. He seems to think he should call the shots, not just give legal advice. To be blunt, the fucker is getting too big for his fancy britches. The guy is an elite, not one of us. He has never gotten his hands dirty selling coke, dealing with turf wars, he never grew up in poverty like we did. He went to fancy schools and moves in elite circles with rich, fancy friends. He is not from the streets of Medellin like us. We don't need him and we especially don't need him trying to be our leader."

"I don't know," said Alfaro, "he's made some good suggestions and got us out of a tough situation with *Los Urbanos*. He was the guy who found a stud of an assassin to take out Lucero, the guy who made them successful, and who took out those L.A. gangbangers who were selling their coke. Bonilla has been an asset."

Others in the room nodded their heads. Escalante merely sipped his scotch in silence as the door to the suite opened and Bonilla, late as always, stepped in.

After pleasantries and brief gossip about the other cartels they got down to business. "I think it's simple, you catch the guy stealing from us he's got to go. Anything else sends the wrong message," said Zaragosa.

The others nodded assent.

"Bonilla, your assassin operates in the U.S., right? Can we get him to take down Morales? How much does it cost us?"

"Yes, using him is probably the right move. If we send someone from Colombia to New York it might attract the wrong attention and he might have trouble getting out after the hit. My guy seems to get in and out of places with no trouble. He probably is an American himself. Morales is a tough hit. He camps out in Spanish Harlem well protected by bodyguards. It's no piece of cake to take him out. Our guy's usual price is fifty K U.S. For this one it is going to be at least seventy-five maybe one hundred."

"Okay, look we give you authority up to one hundred. It's worth it to get rid of the thieving scum. Any more than that and you come back to us," said Zaragosa looking around the table.

The nods of the others told him he had their approval.

"When that sucker goes down, I say we meet and down a case of champagne," said Escalante.

He decided he was going to handle Bonilla himself since the others did not want him gone. Escalante did not have the services of a fancy assassin like Bonilla did but he knew some tough guys in Medellin who wouldn't mind taking out some arrogant fat cat of a lawyer.

Chapter Eight
New York City, NYPD Headquarters, 1 Police Plaza

Marcie Quinn did not look like an FBI agent, even to Becky Haden. She obviously took a lot of trouble with her appearance layering on lots of make-up and enough eye make-up and fake lashes to look like a kewpie doll. Despite all the make-up, Quinn could almost pass for a high school senior. She was a diminutive five foot two with light brown hair done in a flip. She had huge blue eyes. She wore a dark blue pleated skirt with a white cotton blouse and a chain necklace with a heart pendant and strappy patent leather stiletto heels. *If I'm detective Barbie*, thought Haden, *this one out does me ten times over.* Yet, somehow, Haden found herself instantly liking the girl.

"I have to confess I'm only a little over a year out of Quantico," said Quinn with an ingratiating smile.

"How did you ever get the assignment to go after a serial killer who shot two FBI agents?" queried Haden.

"Well, nobody else wanted it. Eric VanDerlies was not exactly popular in the Agency so it was not really like anybody was hungry for revenge, you know? Plus, a lot of people think it's a wild goose chase and the woman died in Costa Rica so we're just chasing a ghost."

"Did Assistant Director Peterson explain why we believe the woman was not killed in Costa Rica? The blood we found was not the same blood type as her birth records. The whole thing was a ruse to put us off her trail. Plus, we have two positive eyewitness IDs for her in a murder that just happened here in New York and a positive match to her fingerprints from a California driver's license she took out under an alias. It's her, I know it."

"Okay, Detective Haden, let's assume you're right. Where does that leave us? How do we find her when there doesn't seem to be a trace of her anywhere on the ground? She may not be dead but she is a ghost."

"Call me Haden, or even Becky if you like. I have an idea if you're ready to get started. Are you with me?"

"Sure, Becky, you're the expert on this case, you take the lead."

"Just before the shoot-out at the Marina where we thought this woman got shot there was a mass killing a few miles south in a place called Dominical. The victims were a bunch of hard-core Colombian drug runners from a cartel called *Los Urbenos*. Costa Rican authorities assumed they were shot by a rival cartel and discounted the possibility that our girl was the shooter."

"Why is this important?"

"First, I am pretty sure that our girl really was the shooter. She's a professional and it was no coincidence that she was there. Besides, she as much as told me she was there to do a job."

"That's right, you actually met this woman."

"I did. The only job that was done in that area that might have required a professional killer was the massacre in Dominical. Costa Rica is not exactly the murder capital of the world and nothing else happened there. So, she is working for a rival cartel that wanted these guys dead."

"I'm with you but how does that help us?"

"The Colombians are busy in the U.S. If we can figure out who she works for and who might be her next victim, maybe we can head her off and be there when she tries to make the hit."

"Makes sense but how do we do that?"

"We start by going to the Narcotics division and seeing what they know about Colombian activity in New York and who the cartels might be interested in seeing dead."

"Sounds good to me," said Quinn.

Haden walked them upstairs to Narcotics. They went to the desk of Detective Luis Padilla.

"Hey, Haden," said Padilla looking up from a pile of paperwork on his desk. "What brings you up to the low rent district?"

"Luis, this is Agent Marcie Quinn from the FBI. Agent Quinn, this is Detective Padilla, the rising star of NYPD's Narcotics division."

Padilla looked at Quinn appraisingly as if he found it difficult to believe she was really an FBI agent. Haden suspected it was a reaction

Quinn frequently received. "We want to know about a group called *Los Urbenos* and who might want to tangle with them."

Padilla nodded. "*Los Urbenos* is a Colombian cartel formed from the remnants of a right-wing militia that fought for the government in Colombia's civil war against the FARC guerillas. When FARC signed an armistice with the Colombian government these boys decided to take over FARC's cocaine labs and started producing product. They lacked a distribution network and began to develop one first in Florida then in New York and L.A. Their main competitor is the Medellin cartel. This is a group formed a few years back from an alliance of smaller cartels that were left over after Pablo Escobar went down. Medellin is very active in the U.S. relying mostly on gangs for distribution."

"So, *Los Urbenos* were encroaching on Medellin territory?" interrupted Quinn.

"Precisely," said Padilla. "*Los Urbenos* began to run into trouble, first in L.A. where the gang that was running their powder got hit hard with their leaders being knocked off. The next blow they suffered was their leader, Marcos Lucero, getting snuffed along with his body guards in Costa Rica. There was no immediate successor being groomed."

"That is why we are here," interposed Haden. "The case we are working on involves the assassin who knocked off Lucero."

"You know who did that?" asked Padilla.

"Yes, we, I mean I, am positive we know who did it. She also killed two FBI agents which is why Agent Quinn is here."

"She?"

"Yes, a professional killer we think is working for a Colombian cartel. From what you have told us it probably is Medellin. What we need to know is where would Medellin be likely to next need a professional killer? Is there someone on their radar? If we can find out we might be able to spring a trap for this girl."

"We just may be able to help you with that, Detective Haden, it will take a little more digging but I'll get back to you as soon as we've got something."

Chapter Nine
Viejo San Juan, San Juan Puerto Rico

Arturo Escalante liked to stay in the old section of San Juan on those rare occasions when he had to go to Puerto Rico on cartel business. He refused to set foot in the continental United States even though there were no warrants out for him. He just felt safer in a Spanish speaking community that did not feel like the United States he saw on television or the movies. He loved staying at the Hotel El Convento in a three hundred-fifty-year old building that was once a convent for Carmelite nuns. The narrow cobblestone streets flanked with sixteenth and seventeenth century buildings reminded him of the old section of Cartagena in his native Colombia where he now often vacationed. He knew the DEA was not particularly active in Puerto Rico, certainly less active than in Florida or New York, which he hated for its bad weather and grim architecture.

Escalante loved to walk along the *Paseo De La Princesa,* especially the part that meandered beside San Juan Bay under the old city walls. Here there were benches where one could stop and watch the cruise ships steaming into the harbor, hear the lapping of the waves and smell the musty odor of the ancient city walls. He sat down on one of those benches and watched a large, white multi-layered cruise ship enter the bay like a floating wedding cake. He was in San Juan to meet with a man who was to become the new distributor in New York City once Alfonso Morales, the current distributor, was taken care of. Bonilla took responsibility for that. Escalante was glad he aired his problems with Bonilla to the rest of the cartel members even though they had not agreed to do anything. He took steps to find the right man to take Bonilla out though he had not come up with him yet. When it happened the other cartel leaders might be upset but at least they would understand why he did it. Eventually they would be grateful.

It was hot but a cooling breeze blew off the water. The salty smell of the ocean filled his nostrils. Medellin, where he was born, was far from the sea. Every time he encountered the ocean it seemed magical. *"No es hermosa?"* said a musical woman's voice in Spanish.

The woman who sat down next to him on the bench was quite lovely herself. Her long, black hair was silky, her skin pale, her large eyes a shimmering shade of pale blue. She wore a white cotton sun dress with dark blue vertical lines and carried a large, dark blue Dior leather purse. "My name is Maria," she said smiling as he turned to look at her.

"Arturo," he replied returning her smile, she was, after all, very pretty. "Your accent is different. Where are you from? You are not Puerto Rican."

"I'm from Panama, Arturo. I would guess you are Colombian, am I right?"

"Indeed. You do not sound like any Panamanian I have heard."

"Perhaps you have not heard many Panamanians. Anyway, I was educated in Spain and the United States so that may be why I sound different."

"So, what are you doing in Puerto Rico, Maria?"

"I came to meet you," she said smiling.

"Ow, what was that?" he said at the feel of a sharp prick in his thigh.

The girl got up and took a few steps away from him.

"That, Arturo Escalante, was a message from Carlos Bonilla and your associates in Medellin. They would rather keep Bonilla and lose you since you two cannot seem to coexist."

Escalante felt his heart racing as if it were about to explode. He suddenly could not breathe. His heart stopped abruptly then began racing again. He fell to his knees clutching his heart. He was unable to speak.

"You picked a lovely place to die Senor Escalante," she said as she tossed a hypodermic syringe into the water, picked up her purse and walked away.

Chapter Ten
Metropolitan Correctional Center, Manhattan

The young African American man sitting across from Elise was twenty-nine years old. His education ended at the seventh grade. He never knew his father and his mother was a crack addict in and out of jail and rehab programs. He had an extensive criminal record of petty theft and drug sales. His arms were completely covered with elaborate and colorful tattoos. He was being held for charges related to being part of a conspiracy to smuggle cocaine and heroin into the country. He was in the lower tier of conspirators and thus far refused to provide any information about the top organizers of the conspiracy. He was facing a minimum sentence of twenty years in Federal prison.

Elise was tasked with evaluating his fitness for trial and his potential for violence. Should he be convicted, as seemed likely, her evaluation would help place him within the federal prison system. Given his record, and if Elise were honest with herself, his race and economic status, he had no chance of going to a low security prison. "Caleb, can you tell me why you left school so early?"

"Ain't no reason to stay. My momma she been arrested for crack, you know, and there be no food on the table and no one to pay the rent. So, I quit school and go to work for this guy fencing stolen goods. He got me shoplifting at first then break-in burglaries, right? School was boring but this stuff it made me some money and I could eat, you know? That's why."

"So, you were taking things that didn't belong to you. Did you ever reflect on how that might be wrong, that someone might be hurt by what you were doing taking their property?"

"Way I look at it I got no choice. Ain't no one looking out for me. No jobs for no thirteen-year-old, moms in jail, I got a little sister who needed to eat just like me. What was I supposed to do? Didn't want no foster care. Man, I got friends who went through that. It's just a different kind of hell. So, I take some stuff. I don't never hurt nobody."

"What about the drugs you sell? Don't they hurt people sometimes?"

"No one be forced to buy drugs, right? I mean if they want them, they get them, if not from me from someone else. It's their decision to buy the drugs and use them, I'm just makin' a buck takin' advantage of that decision. Way I see it they responsible for their own actions, not me."

"So, you don't feel any guilt at all?"

"No. If there was another way to make a buck, I mean I'd do it but you like me, no family, no money no skills, no education, you got few choices. You do what you need to do. I ain't got the luxury to feel guilty."

Elise nodded and made a note. Caleb had good grades in school before he dropped out. He was clearly intelligent. He did not have a history of violence and seemed to take pride in the fact that he did not. She saw him as someone who had a chance to rehabilitate. In the federal prison system, a young Black man with a criminal record was not going to get the chance to meaningfully rehabilitate. She sighed. Sometimes she found working with these inmates and arrestees to be depressing. In so many cases they reflected a distorted and unbalanced society. To make things worse they were not even usually very interesting as case studies. Caleb, for example, was not mentally ill, not a sociopath despite his many crimes. In some respects, he was normal despite his grim circumstances. He could be encouraged to take advantage of the few opportunities prison offered but more likely he was going to be emotionally disfigured by his prison experience. If it weren't for the generous paycheck her prison gig offered, she would quit the assignment today.

She carefully completed paperwork opining that Caleb was non-violent. She recommended a low security prison for him, the sort of place that stock-brokers and bankers went to. Financially his crimes were much less than most of these white-collar criminals. His involvement with drugs and his race would likely motivate prison administrators to ignore her recommendation to put Caleb someplace where he did not belong. Someplace that would likely change him in ways that were not good for him or society.

Chapter Eleven
New York City Community Hospital

It was almost midnight when the power went down. There were two emergency surgeries taking place and several patients on life support in the ICU. Initially, the lights flashed off then came back on when the emergency generator kicked in. The nurse in surgery noticed the life support data on the surgery computer was blank. The lights flashed off again.

At her home, hospital administrator Jennifer Flanagan received a text on her cell phone from an unknown number: *All systems at Community Hospital are currently down due to a virus we have placed in your computer system. If you send one hundred and fifty thousand dollars in cryptocurrency to the account listed below all hospital systems will be restored and your patients will no longer be in danger.*

Immediately, her cellphone began ringing with the night supervisor in a panic asking for direction. Her immediate instructions were to get all ICU and critical emergency room patients transferred to other hospitals as soon as possible. She quickly got on the line arranging beds at alternate hospitals and obtaining transportation. Once these arrangements were made, she got on the phone with the chairman of the hospital board to see about paying the ransom.

Before the cryptocurrency could be transferred one of the patients in surgery died before she could be transported to another hospital. Flashlights and temporary generators brought in by the NYPD emergency crew helped keep most of the patients alive and those in the worst condition managed to find beds in neighboring hospitals before their conditions worsened too badly.

At nine in the morning on the following day the hospital board authorized the payment, the cryptocurrency was sent and within a half hour the systems came back. Flanagan was paid a visit by two government officials. An FBI agent named James Hart and a CIA operative named Cecily Gleeson sat down with her over coffee in her kitchen.

"I don't understand why the CIA would be interested in a hospital hack," she asked Gleeson, a small blonde woman with large dark eyes dressed in a flannel skirt and blue cotton blouse.

"We believe that these hacks are state sponsored, acts of aggression involving foreign governments hostile to the United States. I'm not at liberty to say a whole lot more than that. We have computer experts working on identifying how your network was hacked and where it might have originated but we have a pretty good idea of who might be behind this. We're going to find a way to stop this from happening again," said Gleeson.

Within a few days the government computer experts generated a report, a copy of which, stamped "CONFIDENTIAL" crossed Flanagan's desk. A virus implanted in an e-mail directed to a clerk in the billing department infected the hospital system. The e-mail promised a twenty percent discount on designer accessories and purported to contain a coupon to a high-end clothing store. The virus gave control of the entire hospital network, including climate control, life support equipment and monitoring systems to a remote location locking out the hospital controls. The cryptocurrency used to pay the ransom was untraceable.

Chapter Twelve
New York City, NYPD Headquarters, 1 Police Plaza

Haden and Quinn were going over the case files for Ariella Blumkin when Detective Padilla rang from Narcotics. "I think I've got something for you, why don't you come up here if you have a minute."

Narcotics Division was on the eleventh floor above homicide on the ninth. It was a warren of cubicles in the center of the floor with interrogation rooms and private offices around the perimeter. Padilla's cubicle was close to the elevator. It contained a grey metal desk and a four drawer metal filing cabinet. On the desk was a pile of manila folders and a framed picture of an attractive dark-haired woman with a six-year-old boy. They sat down on tipsy metal chairs across from his desk. "You were asking about Medellin and who they might want to kill next. Well, I may have something for you," said Padilla. "The main distributor in New York for Medellin cocaine is a group called NETA. It originated in Puerto Rican prisons and soon began to take over the streets here in New York, especially in the Bronx and Brooklyn. They call their subgroups *pueblos*. The most powerful *pueblo* in New York is the Bronx *pueblo* run by a guy named Alfonso Morales. They are the primary purveyors of Colombian cocaine in the city. These guys have made a lot of money for Medellin and they are very bad-ass."

"So, who would Medellin want to kill if they have been so successful?" asked Haden.

"Morales himself, because the dude has been skimming. At least that's what our confidential informant tells us. He has been underreporting sales to the Colombians and keeping a bigger cut for himself to the tune of almost a half million a month."

"That's a lot of money," said Quinn "but it still seems like a big risk. If he gets caught, he's a dead man."

"That's right," answered Padilla. "He has a large well-armed crew. Maybe he thinks he's protected. Plus, what we hear is that he has a girl friend who is pushing him hard to make big money. She wants to leave the Bronx and she wants to live large."

"What a man will do for a woman, what fools," laughed Quinn.

"I wouldn't know," said Haden. "Anyway, how did Medellin figure out what Morales was up to?"

"Actually, it was pretty simple," said Padilla. "They knew how much they were shipping to NETA and the returns did not reconcile with the amounts they were sending. Morales was reporting sales that were less than the supply he was receiving and when confronted he couldn't account for the difference. Either he was skimming cocaine or money. Either way he is in big trouble with the cartel. So, you think this girl assassin you are hunting killed Lucero in Costa Rica and maybe will get the call to knock off Morales?"

"That's exactly what I'm thinking," said Haden. "If they hired her to get Lucero and Morales is a difficult hit then she would be the logical choice to get him as well."

"Except I would guess Medellin has more than one hired killer on their payroll. They might even try someone from Morales' own gang. There's no certainty they'll use the girl, right?"

"Okay, so it's a gamble they will use her and not someone else. Either way we end up getting a killer if you really think they will go after him."

"What do we do now?" asked Quinn.

"We start doing surveillance of Morales. Maybe Narcotics can help and maybe we can use some FBI resources?" Haden asked.

Both Padilla and Quinn nodded affirmatively.

"We try to tighten up entry at local airports giving a physical description of our girl to Customs and Immigration warning them she may be entering under an assumed name."

"What if she is already in the country?" asked Quinn. "You seem to be assuming she will be coming in from outside the country. She's an American citizen. You seem to think she may be living in Los Angeles."

"We've got enough now to get an arrest warrant on the Dorsey murder. We get the warrant and put out an APB on her now that we think she may have reason to be back in New York. If we get lucky maybe we get her before she can kill anybody," said Haden.

Chapter Thirteen
Rezdora Restaurant, New York City

Elise had not intended to end up on a date with another finance guy after having been unhappily married to a Goldman Sachs broker. His Tinder profile had been irresistible. Thirty-four, six foot two, one hundred and ninety pounds, jet black hair slightly graying at the temples, plays tennis, loves Russian drama, Dostoyevsky, Kafka and Iris Murdoch, a gourmet cook, the guy was too perfect to be true. That, of course, was the problem, it was not true. Sitting at a table in Rezdora his conversation was as bland and predictable as the middling Italian fare the restaurant served. He was, handsome, tall, fit with an angular profile. She had been won over by looks before and that got her two years of a miserable marriage. They were just past the first course and she was ready to go home.

"So, exactly what is it you do?" he asked politely as if he were interested.

"As I mentioned I'm a clinical psychologist engaged in therapy. I help people with psychological problems."

"Didn't you say you worked in a prison or something?"

"Yes. I have a private practice and an office in Manhattan. I also go twice a week to the Metropolitan Correctional Center. It's a federal prison which handles a lot of federal defendants being held for trial. They want to get a professional evaluation of what level of incarceration is appropriate; whether or not the prisoner is dangerous, has mental or emotional issues that could cause problems around other inmates and would require treatment. Sometimes a criminal defendant tries to use the insanity defense and I'm qualified to evaluate that issue. Occasionally, I'll even testify in court."

"Sounds interesting."

"Sometimes it is. You know a lot of times these are just poor, undereducated people who are ground down by the system. They have limited options, drugs, theft, those are more readily available to them. Race, lack of education, lack of opportunity, all these things keep people down and it's not surprising they turn to crime especially when they see all the wealth surrounding them."

Her date frowned. He obviously disagreed with her but was trying to be polite about it. "I don't know, Elise. A lot of these people are just lazy. The opportunities are there for anyone. School is free. If you work hard, get good grades there are scholarships. I get that it can be tough for some but they take the easy way out ripping other people off, selling drugs that kill people or at least make them addicted. We had a Black president so how does race keep someone from making it in the legitimate world? We have Black brokers at the firm, they make good money but they had to work to get there."

Elise did not want to argue with him. It wasn't worth it.

"Well, we obviously disagree on this and, I suspect, a great many other things. Look I'll leave you some cash to pay my share of the bill but I'm going home. Nice to meet you but it's obvious this isn't going anywhere and I doubt we'll meet again."

With that she grabbed her purse, got up and left.

Chapter Fourteen
The Bronx, New York

Alfonso Morales lived in an eight-story brick apartment building on Southern Boulevard in the Longwood section of the Bronx. He and his homies rented the entire eighth floor. He knew he had problems with Medellin so he surrounded himself with gunmen from his *pueblo*. For the immediate time he felt safe. No one was going to get to him here. The bigger question was where to go in the future. Medellin stopped the flow of cocaine, spreading it to other *pueblos*. Ultimately, he needed to leave. His choice would be to go to Puerto Rico where he had family but his girlfriend, Elena, did not want that. Her choice was the south of France where their money could buy them luxuries unheard of in Puerto Rico. Alfonso was not sure about that but he had become used to doing what Elena wanted.

Their apartment was three bedrooms, two bathrooms, a veritable palace for Longwood. There was one gunman in the apartment night and day, an arrangement that Elena complained about. The two other apartments on the eighth floor were occupied by three gunmen in each. The security, while necessary, was expensive. He and Elena were sick of being stuck inside. Something was going to have to be done soon. They could not go on like this much longer. Maybe Elena had been wrong about skimming money from coke sales. The cartel had caught on quickly. They told him to give it back. Elena said if he did, they would still come after him so he might as well hold out. How much clout could those guys have in New York City?

Chapter Fifteen
Villa Dupleve, Guadeloupe, French Caribbean

Every afternoon the rains came. Hard, driving tropical rain cascading down her stairs to the beach like a waterfall, gushing in torrents from her rain gutters. Ariella loved it. Chet Baker played softly on her stereo. It was an early piece with Russ Freeman on piano and some Italian guy on bass. She marveled to think he had spent much of his early years in the same town in Los Angeles as she did. He even went to the same junior college. Now dead, the trumpet player who exuded those gentle, melodic tones was known as a monster. Drug addict, woman abuser, cheat and liar but musician extraordinaire.

She sat on her couch sipping champagne listening to the monster's sweet trumpet tone as he eased through "The touch of her lips."

Lots of his songs were about love, often lost or hopeless love. She wondered if Baker had ever actually been in love himself. She doubted it. For herself she had never felt love, had no idea what it felt like. Was it always sad? Was there always loss? Could it really make you deliriously happy? She had no idea.

She never felt strong emotions. Not love, not anger, not rage, jealousy or sorrow. Her first relationship was with a Russian literature professor. She did not love him but enjoyed his company and the prestige of being in the company of a bright, handsome, older man. When he dumped her, she felt no rage, merely the calm certainty that he must pay a price. So, she killed him. Not out of rage or vengeance, just a vague, coldly emotionless sense of justice.

Her latest boyfriend was a naïve, nebbish, third rate attorney. Handsome in a disheveled sort of way. She enjoyed his company but when he had trouble adapting to her method of making a living, she dispatched him with only mild regret. That was how she lived. For her the drama occurred in other peoples' lives.

As Baker launched into "Do it the hard way" scatting between trumpet solos, she checked her office, champagne glass in hand. In her e-mail a message offered her a job in New York killing a cheating drug dealer. The compensation offered was sixty thousand American dollars. She countered by offering to kill Alfonzo Morales for one hundred thousand. Within minutes an e-mail arrived accepting her counter offer. Not long after she received e-mail confirmation that fifty thousand had been deposited in her Cayman account. She smiled. Medellin really wanted this guy dead. However, before she could take care of mister Morales, she owed corporate America a visit to Honduras.

Chapter Sixteen
New York City, NYPD Headquarters, 1 Police Plaza

Between the Homicide and Narcotics divisions and the FBI twenty-four-hour surveillance was set up on the Southern Boulevard apartment building which Alfonzo Morales rarely left. The surveillance crew was on the look-out for a woman in her late twenties with striking blue eyes, about five foot seven inches in height weighing approximately one hundred and forty pounds with hair which could be any shade from jet black to red based on her prior disguises. They put out a federal all-points bulletin at airports but since they had no idea where she might be coming from or what passport she might be using they had little faith that TSA or immigration would spot her. The Southern Boulevard surveillance was their best chance. If the Ariella woman was to take Morales down, she needed to come to the Bronx because Morales was showing no sign of leaving his nest.

They established a command center in the NYPD Narcotics division with phone and radio contact with the surveillance team on duty. A week of surveillance provided ample information about Morales' operations and his set up at the Southern Boulevard residence. Morales had always been careful not to use phones to conduct business being afraid of wiretaps. His chief distributors came in person every few days to get instructions and bring cash from collections. Some of them were not previously known to Narcotics and Padilla launched several operations to track them and seize drugs. Even if Morales figured out that he was being watched and that his operations were being compromised as a result, he would be reluctant to leave the security of the Longwood building and risk exposing himself to the wrath of his former Colombian bosses.

The sparse traffic at the apartment building exposed the fact that Morales' operations were suffering. His sources for drugs were drying up now that Medellin refused to ship to him. The recent operations conducted by Padilla helped reduce the sparse drug supplies Morales had left. He was paying a small army to protect him. How long before the money ran out and his bodyguards quit? Were his assassins waiting to smoke him out or starve him to make their hit on him less challenging? If so the surveillance on the Southern Boulevard building might entail a long wait. Haden wondered just how long she could expect her bosses to sustain such a manpower heavy operation.

Chapter Seventeen
Tegucigalpa, Honduras

Ariella peered out the window of her first-class seat as the plane descended to Tegucigalpa. The capital city of Honduras was nestled in a deep valley amongst green clad mountains. She had been here before.

Her first trip was on behalf of the same client as her current journey. Her target had been a middle-aged woman, an indigenous activist who was leading opposition to a major hydroelectric project erecting a dam on a river which served as home for generations of Honduran indigenous people. She was an easy target, with no security, no ability to protect herself and few friends in the capital. Ariella slit her throat and happily collected the easiest fifty thousand dollars she ever earned.

Alejandro Maduro was an entirely different problem. A member of one of the elite twenty-five families who owned and controlled Honduras he served as Minister of the Interior. Maduro was not blocking the hydroelectric project out of environmental idealism or concern for the indigenous community. He was withholding his approval for a very large bribe. A bribe so large that her client determined it was more cost-effective to pay her to kill him than pay what he was asking. As a man of wealth and power he would not be an easy target.

Ariella collected her carry-on bag and walked through airport corridors to immigration where she showed her French passport in the name of Marie Tremblay. She took a cab to the Marriott. When she was working, she tried to stay at large, anonymous hotels where she could blend in without attracting attention. The Tegucigalpa Marriott, a twelve story, one hundred and fifty-three room concrete and glass monstrosity a short drive from Toncontin Airport, was just right.

After checking in she unpacked her bags and disassembled the metal frame of her carry-on bag. The tubular frame was lined with lead foil. She shook the tube and a stainless-steel switchblade tumbled out. She tossed the blade in her purse, then arranged for a car rental through the hotel front desk. Using the GPS on her phone she drove through the broken streets of Tegucigalpa to Maduro's home in the *Colonia Palmira* neighborhood. She passed through neighborhoods of brightly painted cement block shacks with corrugated metal roofs. On street corners gangs of tough young men in khaki pants and sleeveless white tank tops loitered glaring at the nicest cars driving by. There were *carnicerias* and *panaderias*. There was a smell of charcoal and human feces in the air that rolling up the car windows could not displace. In some neighborhoods young girls in short skirts or hot pants and spike heels gestured at the passing cars offering their services.

Maduro lived in a modern district of large multi-story buildings with tile roofs and balconies with elaborate wrought iron railings. Each house was surrounded by a wall with a metal or wooden gate. Many of the homes had conspicuous guards carrying rifles and holstered pistols. Maduro's home was a four-story white stucco affair. The arched windows were barred. The exterior wall was eight feet high with shards of broken glass sticking out of the top and a large metal gate. Ariella parked her rented Corolla across the street. While she sat there a large, black BMW sedan pulled up to the gate which rolled open. A man in a khaki uniform with an AK47 stepped out and exchanged words with the driver. The car drove in and the gate closed behind it.

In a country as violent as Honduras Maduro would likely travel accompanied by a body guard in a bullet proof car. His home was a fortress. Her only chance to do the job was to catch him in a place where he was alone but felt safe. She decided to follow him and take advantage of the first opportunity that presented itself. Maduro himself showed up a few hours later in a dark blue Bentley driven by his security guard. Nothing much happened after that and at ten P.M. she returned to the hotel.

She did not return until four-thirty the next night. She wore a black silk, sleeveless dress that she felt was formal enough to get her into most places where Maduro might go on the chance he went out that night. As on the previous night his Bentley arrived at the house about six. She waited patiently after that. There were few pedestrians so she attracted little attention sitting in her car on the street.

At seven-thirty that night the Bentley slipped out the gate and she followed. The Bentley pulled up at the Hotel Clarion in central Tegucigalpa. Ariella parked the corolla on a side street and hurried to the hotel in time to see Maduro and his wife meet another couple in the lobby and proceed to the hotel restaurant *Las Cuatro Estaciones.* They checked in with the maître d and were ushered to a table.

Ariella approached the reception station "I'm meeting my *novio* tonight, I am so sorry we have no reservations but would you have a table for two?" she asked in Spanish while smiling and batting her eyelashes.

The maître d smiled back and gestured for her to follow. The restaurant was a large open room with windows looking on to the street and a bar on one side. From her table she could see Maduro, his wife, and the other couple across the room. Ariella ordered a drink.

She watched carefully until Maduro excused himself and headed toward the restrooms. She followed, slipping on a pair of nylon gloves as she walked. She waited until Maduro entered the men's room then followed him in quickly looking around to see if there was anyone else present and slipping a wooden block under the latch to keep anyone from entering. Seeing no one she approached Maduro as he faced a urinal. He was a short, stocky man in his mid-fifties with frizzy gray hair trimmed short and a neat gray beard. He looked at her in surprise. "*Senorita* you are in the wrong facility. Please leave immediately," he said angrily.

"On the contrary, *senor,* how could I resist following such a handsome and compelling man wherever he goes?" she answered as she approached him.

As he hurriedly began to zip up his fly, she grabbed him from behind and expertly slit his throat.

With some effort she dragged him into a toilet stall and positioned him on the seat carefully managing to avoid getting blood on her dress. She closed the stall door then went into the next stall and flushed the gloves and switchblade down the toilet. Removing the wooden block, she opened the door a crack to see if anyone was outside. Seeing no one she stepped into the hallway heading for the door to the lobby.

She walked back to her car and returned to the Marriott where she gathered her bag from her room, returned the rental car and checked out. She took a taxi to the central bus depot and boarded a night bus to Guatemala City using her French passport when they crossed the border into Guatemala. From the bus terminal in Guatemala City, she took a taxi to the airport and booked a flight to Los Angeles.

Chapter Eighteen
Metropolitan Correctional Center, Manhattan

Elton Harrow was exactly the kind of inmate Elise relished interviewing. A thirty-two-year-old man born in Brooklyn he had just been convicted of kidnapping and homicide. Harrow hinted at other earlier crimes but, on advice of counsel, refused to discuss them further without a deal. The Assistant Attorney General in charge of the case, wisely in Elise's opinion, refused to deal and Harrow received a sentence of life in prison without parole.

She was fascinated by how cold blooded and guiltless he was. One of the two victims he was convicted of killing was a twelve-year old girl. Elise marveled that someone could kill a child and be utterly without remorse. In her graduate classes she studied psychopaths. Now she had the opportunity to study a real one.

These opportunities came about rarely. Most of the prisoners at the Correctional Center were garden variety criminals. Ordinary people for whom circumstances put them in the unenviable position of needing to commit a crime. Thieves, bunko artists, fraudsters, inside traders, financial manipulators, the occasional murderer, or kidnapper. Most regretted their crimes or, at least, were remorseful about being caught. If forced to they could recognize the social evil they committed even if they felt they had valid excuses for their behavior. Not Harrow.

He was brought into her office in shackles by a guard. In prison denim he was a slightly built man in his forties with long prematurely graying hair and a scraggly gray beard. He peered at her through large green eyes which seemed to Elise to be unnaturally bright. He was not nervous at all, unlike Elise.

"Mister Harrow, I am Doctor Elise Bloom. You are here for me to evaluate for sentencing. Nothing you say in this room will be used against you. You may be completely frank with me and it will not work against your interest regarding prosecution for other crimes."

"It may work against my interest with regard to sentencing?" the man asked in a surprisingly smooth mellifluous voice.

"That is correct. My evaluation will help determine what sort of federal facility you get assigned to. To be fair, given the nature of your crimes you don't expect to go to a low security prison, do you?"

"I suppose not. There might even be advantages in the solitude provided by a high security prison and, of course, I am dangerous," he said smiling.

"Do you see yourself killing again if you got the chance?"

"Without doubt, Doctor Bloom," he continued to smile as he spoke, "if there is an advantage to me in taking a life, I'll do so."

"You feel no remorse?"

"I never have."

"Does that imply you have killed more than the two victims you were convicted of murdering?"

"That's a reasonable inference," he said continuing to smile seemingly with genuine amusement, "although I make no admission."

"Am I amusing you, Mister Harrow?"

"Yes, you are, Doctor Bloom. You are trying to understand me and you cannot. I am sure, Doctor, if you killed someone, even by accident, you would feel guilt, remorse, and sadness. So how can you expect to understand someone who does not and cannot feel those emotions? We are like different species, you and I. The emotions you feel are inexplicable to me, totally foreign. I've never felt them."

Harrow was clearly quite intelligent. He seemed to be enjoying this back-and-forth discussion and showed little fear of being assigned to a high security, perhaps even a supermax, prison.

"You are not afraid of what awaits you in prison?"

"I've never felt fear. I am confident I'll be fine wherever I end up. Despite my sentence perhaps prison will not be forever after all."

"That seems overly optimistic, Mister Harrow," said Elise as she made an entry in her notes, "rarely does anyone escape from these places."

"Well, Doctor," he said continuing to smile, "I am nothing if not resourceful."

She looked at him with his glittering eyes and smirking smile then pulled out his medical file. He seemed to be in near perfect health with the exception that his blood pressure was unusually low. He did seem to exude an almost preternatural sense of calm. Here he was in prison denim, in shackles facing a life of confinement and he was the calmer of the two of them. She did note that his denims were blue, not the purple of a dangerous inmate. He had not made trouble or been violent so far since being in custody.

"Do you enjoy killing?"

"I do, very much. What greater power is there than over the life or death of a fellow creature? I feel almost as if when I take a life it makes me stronger as if I absorb the life force of my victim. Does that sound absurd to you, Doctor?"

"Not absurd. I think it's an unusual way to feel. Would you describe it as exhilaration?"

"An excellent word for it, Doctor. I'm pleased you are beginning to understand."

Elise made another entry in her notebook.

"Well, Doctor, have you decided I need to be assigned to the supermax prison?" he asked almost eagerly. "Certainly, you can't expect any rehabilitation on my part. Even if there were, I have a life sentence so my rehabilitation would be pointless, don't you agree?"

"I agree about your rehabilitation. You're right it will never happen but I'll have to think about where to recommend you to be assigned. You're smart enough to keep out of trouble even if you lack a conscience."

Harrow scowled at her and bared his teeth. He got up from his chair and shook his shackles. Elise pressed the button on her desk to summon the guard who appeared immediately.

"I think Mister Harrow is ready to return to his cell," she said.

It was now her turn to smile as she checked the box on Harrow's form to indicate a recommendation to a medium security facility.

Chapter Nineteen
New York City, NYPD Headquarters, 1 Police Plaza

Haden was at her desk when she received a call from the surveillance team on Morales' apartment on Southern Avenue.

"Looks like somebody just went into the building who might be your girl," said the vice on the other end of the line. It was a guy from Narcotics unlucky enough to get the stake-out assignment.

"Describe her," asked Haden.

"About five seven or five eight, dark hair, very light skin, late twenties, attractive. Wearing a multicolored skirt and leather jacket with some colored ribbons in her hair. She went in with a Pedro Gabon, one of Morales' guys. They looked cozy. I've got to warn you we only saw her from the back so we can't be sure. We'll try to get a picture of her from the front on her way out. The way she was entwined with Gabon it may be a while before we see her again."

"What makes you think it's her?"

"Really, at this point it's just a hunch, but from what we can see of her she matches the description and the pictures you gave us."

"Okay, keep us posted."

An hour later a picture was texted to her phone. It was a shot from the front entrance to the apartment building. Pedro Gabon was a short, stocky dark-skinned man in his early thirties with a shaved head and bushy mustache. His arms, shoulders and neck bristled with tattoos. On his arm was a woman at least an inch taller with long dark hair, pale skin and blue eyes wearing a multicolored miniskirt and a black leather jacket. It was Ariella Blumkin.

"What the hell is she doing?" she asked Quinn who was sitting next to her.

"My guess is casing the joint, as they used to say in the old gangster movies. Too bad they couldn't make an immediate ID or they could have nabbed her right there," said Quinn.

Haden got on the phone to the surveillance team.

"Is she still there," she asked.

"Sorry, she gave Gabon a long hard kiss and took off by herself."

"Any indication that Morales has been hurt?"

"No, I think he's okay," said the Narcotics officer. "No way she walks out of that place kissy kissy with one of Morales' bodyguards if Morales is not okay."

"Well, he could be in on it," objected Haden.

"Even if he were there are six other guys on the eighth floor including one in Morales' apartment. They aren't going to let her go if she hurt him. Besides she had no obvious weapon and it would take more than a switchblade to handle all of them. We would have heard gunshots."

"Well, then maybe Quinn is right and she is just scouting the place and she'll be back. It seems like we have the right set-up."

Chapter Twenty
The Bronx, New York

She walked the four blocks from the nearest subway station carrying a leather pool cue case. It was two in the morning. As she approached the building on Southern Boulevard she stepped into a shadowy alcove off the street and unzipped the pool cue case. She pulled out a fully loaded, military style, AR-15 with four more twenty round clips. She jammed the clips into the back pockets of her jeans.

The front door to the apartment building was locked at night but this played perfectly into her plan. She walked to the door, fired several rounds at the lock and kicked the door open. She then immediately ran to the side of the building around to the back entrance.

She waited exactly four minutes, time enough for the bodyguards on the eighth floor to react and head to the source of the shooting. She unleashed a volley of shots at the back door and ran through crouching in firing position. As she planned the six guards not on duty in Morales' apartment ran down the front stairs and were standing in front of the damaged front door, staring. She emptied the rest of her clip at them. Four were killed instantly but two lay on the floor in pools of blood, wounded but still alive. She changed clips and fired a round into each of their foreheads.

Ariella charged up the stairs with her rifle in firing position but no one came to challenge her. On the eighth floor she went to the door Gabon indicated belonged to Morales' apartment, fired at the lock, kicked the door open and stepped aside expecting a volley of bullets. Instead, there was no one there. She kicked open the first bedroom door to find Morales' girlfriend, Elena, naked, cowering in bed with one of Morales' almost nude bodyguards. Neither was armed. She shot each of them in the head and went back into the living room crouching and ready to duck for cover. A shot came from the main bedroom flying wildly across the room and hitting a table lamp.

"Elena," came a panicked shout from the bedroom.

"She's fucking your bodyguard, *puto*," answered Ariella in Spanish. "I guess you don't keep her very satisfied, Alfonso."

He answered with three more wild shots. He had no idea where she was and was not willing to expose himself to get a better shot.

Ariella crept closer to the bedroom door using various pieces of furniture for cover. Eventually the gunshots would attract unwanted attention, even if this was the Bronx, so she needed to end this and get out. She switched the AR-15 to automatic and fired two volleys at the bedroom door. Changing the magazine as she moved, she rushed the door. Morales lay on the floor bleeding, his pistol lying next him. "Greetings from your friends in Medellin," she said as she placed a bullet in the middle of his forehead.

Mission accomplished she headed down the back stairs. She would dispose of the rifle and her gloves in a back alley a few blocks away, walk a few more blocks then take a taxi back to her hotel.

As she walked out the back door of the apartment building a dozen uniformed and plain clothes NYPD officers aimed their guns at her.

"Welcome to New York, Ariella," said a female detective with a blonde ponytail, "you might want to put down that rifle or you could end up like Eric VanDerlies."

Chapter Twenty-One
The Bronx, New York

When the surveillance team on duty saw Ariella approach the front door of Morales' apartment building, they immediately contacted Haden and Padilla. Quinn was asleep on Haden's sofa. They were all on scene by the time Ariella fired open the front door and ran to the back of the building. "Let's get her," said Haden.

"Not yet," answered Padilla, "she's going around the back to catch the bodyguards in an ambush. Maybe they kill her or even better, maybe she kills them and gets Morales. Either way the world loses one very bad human being and we are that much further ahead."

"That doesn't sound right, Padilla. You're saying we just sit here and wait while people get murdered?"

Haden looked at Quinn for support.

"He's right, Becky, we have no dog in this fight. Why should we risk our lives to save a drug dealer or a professional killer? The world is better off without either one of them. We should just wait and arrest whoever survives. Anyone taking bets on who that will be?" said Quinn.

"I have no doubt who comes out of this alive," said Haden. They heard shots from inside the building, probably on the first floor, then silence. A tense few minutes later they heard muffled shots from the eighth floor, then a volley of automatic fire followed by a single shot. "Is our team at the rear of the building in place and ready to go? My bet is she comes out the back."

"Either way we're ready. There's only the two exits so if it's her, we got her," answered Padilla.

"I'm going around the back, are you with me Quinn?"

"Yes ma'am," responded Quinn with a smile.

Haden was right, Ariella emerged from the back door holding her AR-15 to be confronted by armed police. She looked surprised. On command she laid her rifle on the ground and lay prone on her stomach. After she was cuffed and loaded into a custody van, Haden led a group of officers into the building. On the ground floor by the front entrance, they found six bodies oozing blood. Two were shot in the head execution style. The rest had an assortment of lethal wounds, a testament to the woman's excellent shooting and the extreme velocity of the assault weapon she used. There had not been a scratch on Ariella's body when they took her into custody. To have hit six victims without taking return fire would have required not only surprise but rapid, accurate shooting under duress. Haden pondered on the reckless courage of the woman to take on at least six gang bangers and Morales himself all by herself.

"Quite the demonstration of girl power," quipped Quinn, as if reading her mind.

Haden was surprised how unruffled FBI Barbie was by the mayhem around them. The perfectly polished nails and coiffed hair concealed a tough interior.

They went upstairs to Morales' apartment. The first thing they found were the bodies of Elena, Morales' girl-friend, and his bodyguard in the spare bedroom. She was naked and he looked as if he had just pulled on his boxers before he was shot.

"How romantic," said Quinn "I wonder how much Morales knew about this?"

The door to Morales' bedroom was shattered by automatic weapons fire. There were splinters everywhere. Morales lay, face-up over his bed. There were multiple wounds, none fatal, from the automatic fire. His Glock lay on the floor nearby, apparently dropped after he was wounded. The kill shot was to the forehead, Ariella's favorite target apparently. "That's nine murders and we arrested her holding the murder weapon. Plus, the murder of Brandon Dorsey, we have plenty of evidence tying her to that one. That makes ten," said Haden.

Quinn looked at her appraisingly. "I want her transferred to federal custody for the murder of Federal Agent Eric VanDerlies. We'll be willing to accept jurisdiction to take the New York murders to trial. Do you have a problem with that?"

"None at all," answered Haden.

"Good, because you are going to be the key witness in the VanDerlies case," said Quinn.

Haden just smiled.

Chapter Twenty-Two
Saint Petersburg, Russia

They were all sitting around a conference table in one of the office conference rooms. It was Boromir, his boss Vitaly Potalenko and two other hackers, Vladimir Markov, and Sergei Vasylovitch. "How much code do we have to download to freeze the biggest portion of grid possible?"

"A lot," said Boromir. "It's going to be hard to download that much code through a spam e-mail. It's going to look suspicious."

"I have an idea," said Markov. "We've identified three different agencies connected to the grid we want to freeze. What if we send sequential code via spam e-mails to each agency? Once all three are downloaded they can sequence properly and activate. That reduces the amount of code we need to attach to each e-mail. It may take a while for all three sequences to download but it makes it more likely we can disguise them effectively."

Heads around the table nodded in appreciation.

"So, what message can we send that will likely entice someone to open it?" asked Potalenko.

"How about free concert tickets? Just answer a few questions on the attached questionnaire and you are eligible for free tickets to whatever the hottest upcoming concert might be," said Boromir.

"Excellent," said Potalenko, "that seems to work well. Now have we assessed the potential extent of the blackout we cause and the resulting damage?"

This was Vasylovitch's area of expertise.

"The grid we can impact contains the northern part of New York City, Connecticut, New Hampshire, and Maine. It's an impactful area. It will get attention. If the blackout extends for forty-eight-hours, we estimate about two and a half billion dollars in damage to the local economy. Several deaths are likely to result, impossible to estimate since we don't know enough about back-up power sources, but traffic, hospitals, law enforcement and other emergency services will be heavily impacted," said Vasylovitch.

"Good, we'll make an absurd ransom demand, something like fifty million American dollars. The people funding this effort don't really care about the ransom, they just want to spread chaos and undermine confidence in American institutions. If we get any ransom at all it's a bonus. We'll get paid by the sponsor so long as the hack is successful. What is our time line in developing the coding to get this done?" asked Potalenko.

"We need at least six weeks. We want this to work so it has to be perfect," answered Boromir.

Potalenko raised his glass of tea. "To Chaos," he proclaimed.

The others raised their tea glasses and chimed in.

Chapter Twenty-Three
Metropolitan Correctional Center, Manhattan

Marilyn DeAngelo waited in an attorney/client conference room in the downtown Federal prison. Through an intermediary she had been retained to represent a young woman, whom she had yet to meet, about to be indicted for eleven murders, including that of an FBI agent. DeAngelo primarily represented white collar criminals since they were usually the only ones who could afford her. In her early days out of law school she was a federal public defender representing kidnappers and drug smugglers. When she went into private practice a former client recommended her to a mafia kingpin being indicted on racketeering charges. Maybe her Italian last name did not hurt. She managed to get him a favorable plea bargain and her reputation took off. In recent years she found herself representing clients in financial fraud and stock trading cases. She knew the federal system and had good relationships with the U.S. Attorneys who handled the criminal cases. Still, the only reason she was representing this Ariella Blumkin was the fat retainer she was able to pay. The case for her defense was crap.

A woman entered in shackles dressed in a purple denim jump suit. The usual prison uniform for Metro was blue denim. DeAngelo could not remember what the purple signified. The woman herself was striking. She had long, silky jet-black hair in a pale, delicate face. Even without make-up she was stunning. It was hard to believe an elegant beauty like this was charged with the murders of eleven people including an FBI agent.

For a woman in such deep trouble, she was surprisingly calm. "Miss Blumkin, please sit down. I've had a chance to review the indictment. There is a lot of evidence on every homicide they have charged. Given the number and identity of the victims, you are going to have to worry about the prosecution pursuing the death penalty. I'm going to suggest we cut a deal to get the death penalty off the table and avoid a trial. It does mean you are probably going to spend most, if not all, of the rest of your life in prison. Given how serious your crimes and the profusion of evidence I don't think I can do better for you."

"Call me Ariella," the woman said with a smile surprising DeAngelo with her cool demeanor. "I want a trial, I won't plea bargain for a life in prison."

"You have no defense. You were caught red handed with a murder weapon in your hands in the deaths of nine victims. Ballistics confirms the weapon you were arrested with was used in the killing. You left fingerprints on the neck of one victim and were identified at the scene and you shot an FBI agent in front of a New York homicide detective. How am I supposed to defend that? You'll get the death sentence."

"The current president is not conducting executions so maybe it's not that much of an issue," the woman said with an oddly disturbing smile.

"The last president made sure every execution pending was carried out and he may be president again."

"Still, I want a trial. I'll live with the consequences and you'll get paid a lot of money."

"I don't understand. Do you want to die?"

"I consider dying to be preferable to life in prison without possibility of parole. I'm twenty-seven. I have no intention of spending the next fifty or sixty years in a federal prison. It's no life at all. Besides there may still be possibilities for me."

"I can't imagine what those would be unless you're thinking of a possible escape which is just foolish. I strongly recommend against a trial. If you insist, I'll start preparing. I haven't tried a case in almost two years and I have never tried one where the facts are as bad as this one. You will need to add another seventy-five thousand to my retainer."

The woman smiled. "I'll see that the money is wired to your trust account as soon as possible. Look, I understand your advice and I appreciate it. I'm sure you'll do a great job, as good as anyone could. Anything else?"

"That's it for now. In some respects, the less I know the better off

I'll be. I'll be in touch." DeAngelo buzzed for the guard and the woman rose from her seat managing somehow to seem graceful despite the shackles. She gave DeAngelo one of her inscrutable smiles as the guard led her out.

Chapter Twenty-Four
Portland, Maine

The electricity went out about three A.M. All the lighted signs on the main street went out at the same time. Water and sewage pumps went out. Street lights popped off in unison. Most residents were asleep and unaware but when they awakened the digital clocks by their bedsides were winking. Some people had no water. A few found sewage backed up in the streets. Traffic lights were off. Refrigerators and freezers were already beginning to ooze water from frost melt. The hospital was on emergency generators. Gasoline pumps at gas stations did not work. No one could use their TV or radio to get news except the few who had back-up generators. Those who did learned that the black-out was moving south through New Hampshire, Vermont, Massachusetts, Rhode Island, and northern Connecticut. The governors of Maine, New Hampshire, Vermont, and Massachusetts had already declared emergencies.

There was fear that the grid failure could spread to New York City since the electrical grids for all these states were interconnected. Technicians for the various utilities were frantically trying to find a way to restore the grid. The first utility to get the ransom message was Central Maine Power.

Your electrical transmission grid has been compromised along with those of neighboring utilities in adjacent states. The grid can be immediately restored upon payment of fifty million dollars in bitcoin deposited in the designated account. We urge you to collaborate with the other relevant utilities to raise the money. We need not remind you of the catastrophic consequences of grid failure as you are already experiencing them. Sincerely, Evil Corp.

Collaboration by the many utilities would take hours. Although technicians in New York somehow managed to stop spread of the black-out to the city, no one seemed to be able to reverse the black-out where it already prevailed. Frantic phone calls to Federal agencies eventually got to the White House and an emergency session of Congress was called to debate payment. There were those who adamantly opposed paying ransom of any kind arguing it would simply encourage future hacks.

Meanwhile most economic activity in the affected area ceased. Government agencies estimated the losses in the hundreds of millions of dollars per day. Ultimately no one would authorize payment of ransom money out of fear it would encourage future hacks.

After three days of blackout computer technicians in the Department of Homeland Security managed a work around which restored electricity to the area. Angry governors of the affected states demanded action and the matter was referred to state security departments including the National Security Council, FBI, and CIA. No one seemed to have an answer for what to do to stop future problems.

Chapter Twenty-Five
Metropolitan Correctional Center, Manhattan

Elise's office at Met was painted a drab olive green with tan linoleum floors. The furniture was gray metal; a desk, a swivel chair for her, a single gray metal client chair and an empty metal bookshelf. By now Elise was used to its spartan character and did not let it distract her from the inmate interviews she conducted in the stark surroundings.

The file on her desk was fascinating. It described a woman in her late twenties, college educated, graduated with honors, who was accused of eleven homicides including one apparently committed with her bare hands and another of an FBI agent shot in Costa Rica. It was difficult for Elise to imagine what such a young woman must be like. When the guard ushered in a stunningly beautiful raven-haired woman with delicate pale skin and huge blue eyes, she was shocked. The girl was dressed in the purple denim that Met used for its most dangerous prisoners and she was in shackles. "Can you remove the shackles, please?" she asked the guard.

He looked at her quizzically but did as she asked.

"Thank you for that," said the prisoner rubbing her wrists.

Her voice was a musical sounding mezzo-soprano, pleasant and civilized.

"Miss Blumkin," Elise started.

"Please, call me Ariella," the woman interrupted with a charming smile.

"Alright, Ariella. Can we start with the reason for the purple denims? It looks like you were in a fight with another inmate and you hurt her quite badly."

"That's right. She tried to jump me thinking the pretty new girl was an easy mark. I showed her that I wasn't. For that they gave me these lovely purple garments and put me in solitary. I have to say, I quite like solitary. Nice privacy and I don't have to worry about having to hurt somebody who tries to hurt me. My only complaint is I want some books and they won't let me go to the prison library."

"What books are you interested in getting?"

Elise found herself liking this mass murderer. She was lovely and charming. Yet there was something about her that Elise could sense on a subliminal level that made her think the purple denims were the right choice.

"If I could borrow a pen and paper, I could write them down. Maybe you could help me get them? Solitary might not be so bad with some decent reading."

Elise handed her a pen and tore a blank page out of her notebook for her to write on. She briefly wondered if the woman might use the pen to gouge her eye out and try to escape. Although she sensed a potential for violence in the woman, Elise saw that she was too smart to do anything rash or stupid.

As she eagerly wrote Elise took a moment to look at her more closely. She was, Elise thought, one of the most beautiful women she ever met even in prison denims with no make-up. It was very difficult for Elise to picture this woman strangling a man to death with her bare hands.

Ariella finished her list and handed it to Elise. At the very top was *A La Recherche Du Temps Perdu* by Marcel Proust. "I doubt the prison library has this one," said Elise.

"I'd really prefer it in French if there was somewhere I could get it. I've read it in English, the Scott Moncrief translation not the newer one. I've become fluent in French. I've heard it's much better in the original." The woman smiled that charming smile at her again.

"Maybe I can help you with that and some of these other books too. This one by Borges, I don't think that's even available in English."

"Oh, I'm completely fluent in Spanish, Russian too for that matter. My parents spoke it at home. They were immigrants."

This response reminded Elise that they were not meeting to discuss books but to evaluate the woman's fitness for trial and possible placement in the federal prison system.

"Ariella, you are accused of very serious crimes. How do you feel about what you've done? Do you feel any remorse, any grief for the victims?"

"I feel remorse at being arrested, at being outsmarted by that little homicide detective bitch. About killing people? No, I've never felt remorse about taking a life, not that I'm admitting I have," she added with a smile. Elise felt her heart quicken a little at the smile.

"You don't need to worry. Nothing you say here can be used against you. I'm just trying to get a feel for whether or not you are going to be able to go to trial and if you are convicted how we evaluate where you are assigned in the prison system but these sessions are confidential."

"Would you think less of me if I admitted I was a murderer?"

"I have your file in front of me and the evidence is pretty overwhelming that you are a murderer."

"Does that make you think less of me?"

"To take a human life is a serious crime against humanity itself. It's the ultimate taboo. Most societies punish it severely. We can't all be running around taking out our rage on other people. It would be the end of civilization as we know it."

"I don't feel any rage at all. Not everyone kills from anger, Doctor Bloom. Would you mind if I call you Elise?"

This was not something Elise would ever allow in one of these sessions. Doctor patient distance was essential to maintain.

"Yes, of course you can call me Elise." Somehow not wanting to break the rapport she found herself enjoying she broke her own rule regarding familiarity. "If people don't kill out of rage, why do they kill, Ariella?"

"I don't mean to sound glib, Elise, but they kill because they can. Just as with animals some people are prey and some are predators. The predators kill for benefit just like lions, leopards and jaguars do. They kill to eat and feed their young. They don't feel remorse about killing a deer or gazelle, it's just what their DNA programs them to do."

"Don't you think, Ariella, that we are more highly evolved than some jungle cat, that we have built civilizations on cooperation, communal activity?"

"We like to think we are more evolved. Our civilizations depend upon some people exploiting others. There is plenty of killing going on, we have hardly eliminated that."

"So, Ariella, if you are hypothetically one of these superior predators, what are you doing locked up in a cage?"

"Even leopards and jaguars get caught sometimes end up in zoos or other types of cages. Predators are not infallible." She stopped for a moment and looked right at Elise. "You know despite your attempts to hide it you are a very beautiful woman, Elise. It's a huge advantage in life. You should try to emphasize it, not hide it."

Despite herself Elise found that she was blushing.

"Have you ever had sex with a woman?" Ariella asked looking right at her and smiling.

"In my life being attractive has been a detriment. We are getting way off track. Talking about my sexuality is not accomplishing anything."

"It is interesting. You are interesting, Elise. It's been a while since I've had a conversation with an intelligent woman. I quite like it."

Elise felt her heart quicken at that and the palms of her hands becoming moist. She needed to get this interview back on track.

"You realize that the charges against you are very serious. Society views what you have done as intolerable. If you are convicted the punishment will be quite harsh. Do you understand why that would be?"

"Society tries to preserve order and protect the weak from predation. I understand that. The fact that it is not very successful doing so doesn't keep it from being socially utilitarian to make and enforce such rules."

"You break those rules with impunity. Don't you think that's wrong?"

"As a matter of social theory murder is wrong. From a practical point of view for someone like me the benefits are so great that there is no reason for me to worry about social utility. I do what benefits me and no, I don't think that's wrong. Do you think that works as an insanity defense?"

That, of course was precisely why Elise was pursuing this line of questioning. Did Ariella know the difference between right and wrong?

"As a general rule the insanity defense is not allowed for psychopaths or sociopaths although each case has its own unique features.

Has anyone ever diagnosed you as a psychopath?"

"It may have been mentioned a few times by friends and family. The term 'monster' has been used more frequently to describe me. Do you think I'm a monster, Elise?" the smile was still there on Ariella's face. This time she looked genuinely amused.

"I'm not supposed to sit in judgement on inmates. You seem highly intelligent and unusually self-aware. I'm not sure those are things I would expect in a monster."

"Thank you for that. I really do wish I could get to know you better, Elise. I like you."

This time the smile was not amused. It was genuine and directed at her.

"Our time is up," said Elise. "I wish we had more time to spend. I think you are a very interesting woman, Ariella, and I'm sorry you find yourself in such a dire situation even if it was your own actions that got you here."

Ariella reached out and put her hand over the desk on Elise's. she felt a tingling sensation that quite surprised and disturbed her. She rang for the guard who came in, re-shackled Ariella and escorted her out.

Elise was certain that Ariella would not be able to successfully plead legal insanity as a defense. Her notes would reflect that. She also regretfully would recommend that Ariella be assigned to a high security prison if found guilty. As much as Elise liked and, she admitted to herself reluctantly, found her strangely attractive, she knew that the woman was highly dangerous. Despite having drawn these conclusions, which was all she was required to do, she determined that she very much wanted to see the woman one more time.

Chapter Twenty-Six
CIA Headquarters, Langley Virginia

They sat around a metal table in a windowless conference room. Assistant Director Mark Fulham, CIA Russia desk chief Marcie Bernard, agents Nadia Ospina and Cecily Gleeson were arranged around the table along with Gene Falk from the State Department Russia Desk. Ospina had been a liaison at the U.S. Embassy in Moscow for two years. She spoke fluent Russian as did her boss, Bernard. Gleeson had been investigating a series of blackouts in conjunction with I.T. guys from Homeland Security.

"We are finding Russia to be increasingly aggressive," said Falk. "These blackouts come about as close to an act of war as anything they've done so far.

"The pressure from the White House to do something about it is intense. That's why we're here. We have to find a way to stop future blackouts," said Fulham.

"I can tell you that diplomatic pressure has had no effect," said Falk. "Russia simply denies the blackouts have anything to do with them or that they are even originating on Russian soil."

"There can be no doubt," said Bernard, "that the attacks have been launched from within Russia and we have an inside source that tells us the Russian government, through indirect channels, has sponsored and paid for the activity."

"I see our options as very limited." Said Fulham. "If Russia will not acknowledge that they have any responsibility, we can only howl in protest. We know Russia does not embarrass easily. So public accusations have limited, if any, effect."

"What about a covert strike?" asked Ospina.

"Too risky," responded Falk. "If it were discovered it could lead to war. I mean this isn't Pakistan we're talking about."

"What alternative do we have?" asked Ospina. "Besides what if we could not be linked in any way to the covert strike? How does Moscow accuse us of hitting an operation they insist does not exist?"

"Do we know enough about the origin of these hacks to even target a covert strike?" asked Falk.

"I think we do," said Gleeson. "Our I.T. guys have identified a facility in Saint Petersburg as the likely origin of the malware being used. We can get satellite pictures and maybe even agents assigned to the consulate in Saint Petersburg to case it for us."

"How do we dissociate ourselves from involvement if something goes wrong, as it is very likely to do?" asked Falk.

"We use an operative not associated in any way with our security services. Maybe even not American. So, if they are caught, they can't be linked to us in any way. If they get tortured and confess, we plausibly deny involvement and the Russians will have no proof other than a confession under duress," answered Ospina.

"Where would we find someone skilled enough to pull this one off but not linked to U.S. security services?" asked Bernard.

"Once we have approval and authorization to pay someone, we will find one. There are plenty of mercenary types who might take the chance if the pay is good enough," said Ospina.

"That raises questions about a paper trail for payment that might lead to a U.S. agency. We would have to deal with that. Then there is the question of having this person around if they are successful. They will always be walking evidence of American complicity in the covert strike. Blackmail or some other form of revelation might be a problem," objected Fulham.

"I suppose there are work arounds for the payment, maybe using a shell corporation, or simply paying in cash. As to walking evidence I think we know of a way to take care of that," said Gleeson.

"Well let's consider a covert strike as on the table. We need to know a lot more before we can authorize anything like that. Gleeson and Ospina can you work on the details and bring them back to us?" said

Fulham. "Any objections from State?"

"In the absence of other options let's go ahead, take a look to see what we can put together. It's a radical solution but if it worked the Russians would have a hard time complaining about a hit on an operation they claim doesn't exist," answered Falk.

Chapter Twenty-Seven
Le Coucou Restaurant, Manhattan

Elise was having dinner with her best friend Maddie Krug in the elegant dining room of this midtown French restaurant. While toying with her pork liver pate' and cornichons she thought about Ariella Blumkin in her purple prison denim. "Have you ever been attracted to a woman?" she asked Maddie.

"Well, are we confessing secrets tonight? I haven't even finished a half glass of wine yet, but yes, I have found certain women in my life attractive. What about you?"

"I just met a woman, a very beautiful woman, who is the most fascinating creature I've ever met."

"Given your lack of success with men, maybe a little same sex romance might be good for you," suggested Maddie.

"The only thing is, this woman is an inmate at Met. She was arrested for a mind-boggling number of brutal murders."

"You really do know how to pick them don't you, Elise. First a spawn of the devil broker at Goldman Sachs, now a serial killer. I'm just not sure which is worse."

"I'm not physically afraid of her. I really don't think she would ever hurt me. Still, what kind of person kills eleven people with no remorse? Is that someone worth caring about?"

"I'm assuming that's a rhetorical question? Eleven murders are a lot. Even if this woman returned your feelings isn't she going to be in prison for a very long time if not forever? That might make a relationship a bit difficult."

"You're right, it's crazy. I just think my romantic life has been so unsatisfactory lately that my fantasies are running wild and in ways I would have never imagined."

"Maybe this flight of fancy is telling you to explore new avenues.

These days there is no shame in being bisexual or gay, except in evangelical circles. Maybe you just need to find yourself a nice girl friend and stop dating men in the financial sector," laughed Maddie.

"Maybe your right, Maddie. Perhaps I've been looking in all the wrong places. I just don't know how to go about lesbian dating. Is there a girls only version of tinder I could use?"

"I wouldn't know. I've always been straight as a tequila shot so you're hitting up the wrong girl for that."

"I don't know. I'm not sure what I want. All I know is that I'm lonely, frustrated and want to be in a healthy, positive relationship."

"Yeah, like with someone who has murdered eleven people?"

"You know, if she weren't incarcerated, I think I might give it a try. Does that sound crazy?"

"Well, you're the psychologist but, yes, that does sound very, very crazy and maybe just a little desperate."

"The woman is probably about to be shipped off to some high security federal prison somewhere far from New York and I'm the one who is recommending that."

"Elise, you were always very serious about your work and very competent. I'm not surprised that you would not allow a deep crush to keep you from recommending the appropriate level of incarceration for the woman you are sweet on."

"Thanks for your support, Maddie. I do know that I want to see this woman at least one more time before she is shipped off to the hinterlands of the federal prison system even though I have no clinical reason to see her again."

"Good luck with that, sweetie, but try not to let her break your heart or any other part of your anatomy for that matter. Anyway, what's the fish tonight?"

Chapter Twenty-Eight
Metropolitan Correctional Center, Manhattan

Elise felt her palms sweating as she waited for Ariella Blumkin to be escorted in to her office. She appeared in shackles still in her purple denim. Once again, she asked the guard to remove the shackles and once again, he gave her a quizzical look as if she were courting unnecessary danger.

"You look good, Ariella, like you haven't been suffering prison life too badly."

"I'm getting plenty of beauty sleep. I have lost a few pounds. It's impossible to say just how bad the food here is. It's almost not worth eating at all."

"How is your case going?"

"I had to appear and plead innocent, that's about all I've had to do other than meet with my lawyer a few times. Poor thing she's tearing her hair out trying to come up with a defense for me. I feel sorry for her."

"Why did you insist on a trial? I've reviewed your file. The evidence against you is overwhelming. There is a real chance you could get the death sentence. Why not just plead out and take the death sentence off the table?"

"I have my reasons. I'm not discussing them here. My trial strategy is none of your business. I thought we concluded our business at the last interview. Why am I here?"

Elise felt her heart lurch at these words. She decided to be honest.

"You're right. I got everything I needed from you last time. I just wanted to see you again. It may be the last time. I hope I'm not being too forward? If I am I'll call the guard back in and you can go back to your cell. I'm not trying to take advantage of you."

"No, you aren't the type," said Ariella smiling. "I'm glad you called me back. I enjoyed our session last time and I find you attractive.

If circumstances were different, I would ask you to dinner."

Elise felt a release of tension and another feeling she had no words for.

"I'm sorry. I had to recommend against accepting an insanity plea. I submitted a recommendation for you to be assigned to a high security prison. I felt bad about it but maybe it's best for you to be somewhere you have some protection."

"I knew what you would recommend. You were doing your job. My lawyer already explained why an insanity plea wouldn't work. I think I'd be better off in a high security penal facility than a facility for the criminally insane. You don't think I'm clinically insane do you, Elise?"

"No. I'm not sure I understand why you've done the things you've done, why you have no guilt or remorse. I was married to a self-centered, insensitive man but when I left him, I felt bad that I bruised his ego even though I knew I was right to leave him. If I ever physically hurt someone, I am not sure I would ever get over it."

"That's why my own mother called me a monster and that was long before I had done anything like what I was arrested for. My first real boyfriend called me a monster. My second boyfriend was too meek to say it but he wanted to leave me because of the things he saw me do. So maybe they were right and I am a monster compared with someone like you who feels empathy and remorse. Can a monster find love?"

"I don't pretend to understand you, Ariella, but I'm not prepared to judge you. There is something about you that draws me to you."

"Are you sure it's not my looks? I'm aware of how I look. It has opened a lot of doors for me and it has been a kind of camouflage too. No one expects a beautiful woman to be lethal. No one expects a monster to be beautiful."

"It's not just your looks, Ariella. I've only ever been with men so I am not sure what draws one woman to another. I like the fact that we can talk to one another. I appreciate your intelligence and your self-awareness. It is not something I've found in many of the men I've been involved with. I do like you and I don't see you as a monster."

"You really are a talented therapist, Elise. Somehow, I think you've come closer to understanding me than anyone I've known. Thank you for the books by the way. I didn't expect you to follow through on that but they've made my life so much easier. I know I come across as unflappable but prison is hard, it's dangerous. Before I was locked up here, I had a very good life. The only thing I lacked was someone with whom to share it. I can't say now how things may go for me but I have no intention of being locked up for life."

"You're not really thinking of trying to escape, are you? Is that why you insisted on a trial you have no chance of winning?"

"If you knew that to be true, wouldn't you have a duty to report it to the authorities?"

"I suppose I would."

"I refuse to comment other than to say that you are correct that an escape attempt would be very dangerous. On the other hand, prison itself is dangerous."

As Ariella said this Elise's session timer went off.

"I'm afraid we have no more time. We will probably never see each other again. I'll be thinking about you, hoping for the best for you whatever happens."

Ariella got up from her chair and crossed the desk. She bent down and kissed Elise on the lips her tongue slithering into Elise's mouth, her hands on the back of her head. Elise felt a warmth and tingling flush through her body. She wished the kiss could go on forever.

Ariella released her gently. "I guess you need to buzz for the guard," she said.

Chapter Twenty-Nine
Medellin, Colombia

They met in a small Italian restaurant in a back room reserved for banquets. The occasion was the demise of Alfonso Morales, key drug dealer in New York City who was stealing from the cartel. Seated around the table were Roberto Alfaro, Juan Solis, Tasso Almonte and David Zaragosa. Also present was Alberto Solano who had taken the place of the now deceased Arturo Escalante. Solano agreed to the demise of Escalante as a way of keeping peace within the alliance of cartels. It had become known that Escalante was in contact with potential assassins to kill the cartel's lawyer, Carlos Bonilla. The governing board was forced to choose between Escalante, one of the original founders of the alliance which had become the *nuevo* Medellin cartel, or Bonilla. They chose Bonilla and Escalante had been quietly dispatched by Bonilla's assassin in Puerto Rico.

Bonilla himself entered the room and shook hands all around. They ordered a bottle of champagne to celebrate the demise of Alfonso Morales. His successor was already in place and they had already seen increased profits from the lucrative New York market. Morales' demise was not without its own problems.

"As you all know Morales and his bodyguards were slaughtered. However, that was followed by an arrest of the person responsible for the killings. I'll confess that as long as I have used this professional, I had no idea as to their identity. You can imagine how surprised I was when the person arrested turned out to be a young woman," started Bonilla.

"What led to the arrest?" asked Solis.

"As far as we can tell our assassin was wanted for some other murders. It appears that in taking out Marcos Lucero she managed to kill an FBI agent who had been tracking her regarding some other killings in New York having nothing to do with us. The FBI had been tracking her and someone managed to link her to us. Apparently, the NYPD Narcotics folks knew about our problems with Morales," explained Bonilla.

"This presents a real problem for us," said Alfaro. "One of our contract killers in custody could put our whole operation in peril if she talks."

"A problem, yes," said Bonilla. "Not as big a one as you might think. This woman knows nothing about us or our operations. Our dealings with her have been at arms' length. She knows nothing about us, not even my name, just as we knew nothing about her, not even her gender. There simply is not a lot she can tell them about us. I think they already must know she was working for us but they can't prove that."

"Unless she testifies to it," interrupted Almonte as a waitress brought in a magnum of Dom Perignon and a tray of glasses.

The conversation paused as she popped open the bottle and poured the frothy straw-colored liquid into crystal flutes.

"Yes, she can tell them what they already know. That knowledge will not lead to any arrests or disruption of our operations," said Bonilla after the waitress left.

"Even so we should be careful and take steps to ensure her silence," said Almonte.

"Agreed. It is a shame to lose such a talented killer but they usually have a limited shelf life. Right now, she is in solitary but once she is assigned to a facility in the prison system and released into the general prison population, we should have no problem dealing with her. We have contacts in most of the federal facilities that will insure she is silenced for good. My contacts in the New York federal court system will keep me apprised of her trial and ultimate prison assignment. It will be handled, gentlemen, I promise you. Now let us toast to the demise of that cheater and traitor Alfonso Morales."

The men raised their glasses in toast and drank. Satisfied grunts filled the room as they savored their champagne.

Chapter Thirty
Metropolitan Correctional Center, Manhattan

Ariella was lying on her bunk in her narrow cell reading Volume II of *A la Recherche Du Temps Perdu* in the original French. She was already a third of the way through the section titled "The Guermantes Way." Her progress with French had been very satisfactory even without the benefit of a French/English dictionary. She loved the fluent, graceful prose of this gay, half-Jewish writer who always wrote from the point of view of an outsider. She could identify with that perspective very easily.

She was interrupted by a click of the cell door. A male guard with shackles in hand entered. "You have visitors," he said as he approached to apply the shackles.

"Do I have a choice?" she murmured.

"No, this is a mandatory visit. Your presence is required."

After being shackled she was escorted through prison hallways to a conference room like the one where she met with her lawyer.

Two women sat at a metal table. One was tall, blonde, with a long face, long nose, and pale gray eyes. the other woman was shorter, also blonde, with dark streaks in her hair, petite with dark eyes that were almost black. "My name is Nadia Ospina," said the tall one. "This is Cecily Gleeson. We're with the CIA."

"Pleased to meet you," said Ariella in a mock chirpy voice that concealed her extreme curiosity as to why two CIA agents would want to talk to her.

"You have a rather unique history, Miss Blumkin. One that interests us quite a bit," said Ospina in Russian.

"Your Russian is excellent, Agent Ospina," replied Ariella in Russian with the slight Saint Petersburg accent she inherited from her parents. "It is hard for me to imagine what might interest the CIA about me. I agree that my history is unique."

"Just testing your Russian," Ospina said in English. "Out of deference to Agent Gleeson we should continue in English. Your Russian seems quite good and your accent is impeccable."

"I grew up speaking it at home. My parents were both immigrants. While my mother became quite competent in English, my grandfather, who lived with us, never learned so we spoke Russian exclusively at home."

"As did I," said Ospina. "My parents were also immigrants. They were never quite comfortable in English. You mentioned your mother and grandfather. What about your father?"

"He died before I was born so my mother raised us by herself with help from my grandfather."

"It appears your family came to a tragic end while you were in junior college. Can you tell us about that?" asked Gleeson.

"Do I have to?"

"Look, Miss Blumkin, you are in very serious trouble right now, trouble that may very well result in a death sentence. We know who you are, a professional killer, but that's why we're here. If you cooperate with us, we may be able to help you," said Gleeson. Ospina nodded.

"Help me how?"

"Just answer our questions and we will get into that, okay?" said Ospina.

"All right," sighed Ariella. "My family were all killed. My mother, brother and grandfather were all brutally murdered while I was at the school library."

"Did you have anything to do with it?" asked Ospina.

"Are you suggesting I did?" queried Ariella.

"No," said Gleeson, "but we're about to offer you the deal of a lifetime so we'd like to know who we're dealing with. Look, whatever you say to us won't be used against you. You kill people, right?"

"If you've reviewed my file, you know that's what I am accused of."

"Suppose we asked you to make a hit and offered you freedom in return?" asked Gleeson.

"I wouldn't have much choice but to take it, right?"

"Oh, you have a choice," said Ospina. "You can choose to go to trial, get convicted and head to the gas chamber, or if you are lucky, life without parole. You could choose to take our deal, make a hit for us, live happily ever after, a free woman."

"How is this going to work?" asked Ariella.

"First, there are a few strings attached. If you are successful making the hit and are able to escape you can never set foot in the United States again. We don't want you back," said Gleeson. "Your case will be dismissed at the request of the government without prejudice. That means it could be reopened at any time. You know there is no statute of limitations on murder. If you are found back in the U.S. you will be arrested and back in custody as if this deal never took place. Understood?"

"Okay," agreed Ariella.

"We are going to ask you to buy a plane ticket to Saint Petersburg, Russia immediately after you are released. Book a hotel room for three nights, your choice. You will be using your own money. I or someone I designate will meet you there to explain the hit and provide you with a weapon. If you are killed or captured the U.S. will officially disavow any knowledge of any connection to you. If you are successful, I'll give you plans to meet me so I can help you get out of the country," said Ospina. "Do you have a passport you can use, preferably not a U.S. passport?"

"I do. Where will I meet you in Saint Peterburg?"

"Probably in your hotel. We'll figure it out. I may be watched so I need to be careful or I may need to use an intermediary not affiliated with the embassy," answered Ospina.

"What is it I am hitting?"

"Do we have a deal?' asked Gleeson.

"We do," responded Ariella. "I'm all yours."

"Have you heard of 'Evil Corp'?" asked Gleeson.

"They're hackers, right?"

"Very successful hackers. Their offices are in an old palace in Saint Petersburg. The security is minimal. We want you to kill as many hackers as possible and destroy their servers. You'll have a chance to case the main facility but you can't get in without a pass card so you may be operating somewhat blind," said Ospina.

"You'll be released the day after tomorrow. We want you on a plane to Russia as soon as possible. If you try to run the deal is off and you end up back here. We will catch you."

"I'm free to live my life after I make this hit so long as I don't set foot on U.S. soil?"

"You got it," said Gleeson.

"Don't worry about me trying to run. I've done harder hits than this with less at stake."

Chapter Thirty-One
New York City, NYPD Headquarters, 1 Police Plaza

Becky Haden was on the phone with the U.S. Attorney's office. "I just want to know if a trial date has been set yet for Ariella Blumkin," she asked the secretary on the other end of the phone line.

"I'm going to have to get back to you on that, Detective Haden. There has been some delay in that case. The case status may have changed. I can give you a call when we have some clarification," was the response.

Haden was annoyed but assumed that it was just the usual legal snafu and the slow process of the Federal courts that was muddying the water. She was sure a trial date would be set soon or perhaps a plea bargain announced which would undoubtedly put Ariella Blumkin away for life. Haden settled back to reading case reports from the three detectives she was now supervising.

Later that morning Marcie Quinn stopped by. She was still in town temporarily assigned to the New York FBI office while awaiting a new assignment. She and Haden agreed to meet for lunch. As always, the trim agent was dressed to impress in a light blue worsted suit of pleated skirt and jacket, patent leather spike heels and white silk blouse. Her blonde hair was styled in a blunt bob framing her delicate profile. Her nails were done in a pale blue and Haden could smell what she was sure was a faint whiff of Chanel Number Five. As she passed by the desks in homicide, she got ample attention from the mostly male occupants. Haden sighed. Quinn's looks could be deceiving. She was a lot smarter and tougher than she looked.

"Have I had a frustrating morning," she said to Quinn. "I've been trying to get some idea of when the Blumkin trial will be set. I was told she was insisting on a trial and I would have to be a witness regarding Eric VanDerlies' death. I just want to know when I might be free to schedule a vacation. All I get from the U.S. Attorney's office is a runaround."

Quinn grimaced suddenly looking uncomfortable.

"What is it, Quinn? Why the weird look?"

"I don't know if I should tell you but FBI got some information on the trial status. It was because we lost two agents to Blumkin that they felt we needed to know."

"So, tell me," demanded Haden.

"Okay, I know you are as invested in this case as anyone at FBI so when you're ready let's go to lunch. I'll tell you what I know but you have to promise not to repeat a word to anyone. I would be in very big trouble if anyone found out I leaked and I mean more trouble than just losing my job."

Haden nodded and went back to her paperwork while Quinn sat next to her desk and filed her nails. Once she finished the report she had started before Quinn arrived, she grabbed her purse and they went down to a small Italian restaurant a few blocks from police headquarters.

They decided to split a pizza and a pitcher of coke. "All right," said Haden, "what's going on?"

"Homeland Security authorized her to be released to the custody of the CIA," said Quinn.

"What? She's supposed to be tried for eleven murders, including an FBI agent. What does CIA want with her? What about her case?"

"The case is suspended. I have no idea what the CIA could want with her but DOJ is fully behind this whatever it is," said Quinn.

"So, she's out, roaming around?"

"I don't know exactly. She is out of prison but for all I know she is in some sort of CIA black site or something."

"What scares me," said Haden, "is she might make a really good CIA agent. She's smart, she speaks multiple languages, she's adept with weapons and an efficient killer. What if they want her to join up and become an agent?"

"We were assured that eventually they will make sure that Ariella

Blumkin gets exactly what she deserves, what she would have gotten if she went to trial."

"What does that mean?" asked Haden.

"To be honest," said Quinn, "I'm not sure we will ever know."

Chapter Thirty-Two
Saint Petersburg, Russia

Ariella peered out her porthole window as the plane descended through thick clouds to Pulkovo airport outside Saint Petersburg. She changed planes in Munich, Germany after her flight from New York. She was both tired and restless after the long flight.

In New York, just after her release, she met in a coffee shop with Ospina. They agreed she would stay in the Belmond Grand Hotel Europe just three blocks from the offices of Evil Corp. She would pay the hotel bill from her own funds. Ospina arranged a rendezvous for the day after Ariella arrived at which a weapon would be delivered. On the day of the hit, if Ariella managed to get out, she was to take a train from Vitebsky station to the outlying suburb of Pavlovsk where Ospina herself would meet her with a car to take her to a small airfield where a private plane would fly her out of Russia.

"You and I have a lot in common," Ospina told Ariella. "We are both the children of Russian immigrants who left the motherland to escape persecution. We grew up with one foot in the land of our parents and the other in modern America not being fully a part of either one. We were the odd ducks. Am I right?"

"Always the odd duck," responded Ariella. "Now, you are on the home team, an elite agent for a powerful security agency. I'm still the odd duck, not part of anything, living by my wits."

"I don't feel sorry for you," said Ospina. "You've done alright for yourself and now you're out of jail. One job to do and you can melt into the background having gotten away with a bushel full of murders. We've both done okay for a couple of odd ducks."

Ariella used her French passport going through immigration. She breezed through the usually tough immigration police. She was a pretty girl who spoke fluent Russian with a Saint Petersburg accent. She flirted and joked with the officer who processed her passport.

"Are you coming home?" the officer asked noting her accent.

"Just coming to visit relatives. My parents lived here before they moved to France. I still think of myself as Russian though with so many family here."

The Belmond Grand Hotel Europe was a late nineteenth century structure predating the Bolshevik revolution. Parts of it were quite grand but her room was one of the cheapest lacking the vintage charm and antique furnishings of the better accommodations. After all, she was not being paid for this job and had to pay her own expenses, so there was no sense being extravagant. Besides, extravagance could attract attention.

After checking in and stowing her luggage in her room, Ariella strolled the three blocks to the old Vordinsky palace. It was a six story, nineteenth century building. Pantera Corporation, her target, had the fifth and sixth floors. A brief inspection of the lobby indicated a single armed security guard at a desk. Pantera had its own elevator which required a passkey card to work. There were stairs but they were locked from the outside. A review of the outside of the building gave her a few ideas about an escape route, one that would require very sensible shoes.

She went to bed early that night, fatigued from the long flight. The next morning, as arranged, she was seated in the hotel coffee shop at ten. A few minutes after ten a young woman, her hair in a bun wearing thick dark rimmed glasses, came into the coffee shop with a large leather valise. "Are you Ariella Blumkin?" she asked in Russian as she approached.

"I am," replied Ariella in Russian.

"Here are the papers you have been waiting for," said the girl putting down the valise next to Ariella. "I hope it is what you were expecting. Good bye." The girl left as quickly as she entered. Ariella picked up the valise and found it to be quite heavy. She lugged it up to her hotel room. When she opened it, she found a standard Israeli manufactured Uzi submachine gun with a metal, foldable stock and five thirty-two round magazines of nine-millimeter ammunition. Also included were four egg shaped cylinders on short sticks. Ariella recognized them as RGD-5 Russian military grenades.

The Uzi would not have been her choice of weapon. She would

have much preferred a Kalashnikov so she could switch between single shot and automatic. With only one hundred and sixty rounds accuracy was an important consideration. If the Uzi was all she had she would make it work. She suspected the grenades were included for use on the Pantera servers. She had never used them and had only a vague idea how much time elapsed between unhooking the fuse and detonation. She spent the next hour or so inspecting, disassembling, and reassembling the Uzi until it felt familiar and comfortable.

Chapter Thirty-Three
Lucien Bistro, Manhattan

Lucien was not the sort of place Haden would normally frequent, it was Quinn's idea. She had to admit though the food was good and the prices reasonable. Leave it to Quinn, the foodie, to find a place where you could order cassoulet or grilled quail on a law enforcement officer's salary. In the last few months since Marcie Quinn had been permanently assigned to the New York FBI office she had become Haden's best friend. Despite being a very attractive woman Quinn did not seem to have a boyfriend. Haden had not ventured out with a member of the opposite sex since her disastrous and accidental liaison with Eric VanDerlies ended in her pregnancy. Somehow the stress of that whole episode, together with the time demands of her job, made dating seem unappealing and impractical.

"I still get angry when I think about the Blumkin bitch," said Haden between spoonfuls of onion soup. "After being caught red handed killing nine people and overwhelming proof of two more murders she somehow avoids a trial and disappears."

"Assistant Director Patterson was pretty upset about that too but the Homeland Security people who briefed her assured her that the woman would be taken care of eventually," said Quinn.

"Do you believe that?"

"I think I do. My guess is that they wanted her for something. That would be something way above our humble paygrade. You said yourself the woman was a skilled and creative killer. Can't you imagine CIA or someone wanting her to do something the government did not want to be associated with?"

"She belongs in prison or maybe on death row. She's a danger to us all," protested Haden.

"Well, they said she would be taken care of," responded Quinn.

"What does that mean exactly?"

"To be honest I'm not sure. The CIA has a sort of popular reputation for being ruthless. Maybe they mean to kill her?" queried Quinn.

"I think that's mostly in the movies and TV," said Haden. "They are still a government agency and we are still the good guys, right? Good guys don't do extra-judicial murder, do they?"

"These days I'm not so sure who the good guys are any more. Didn't we have 'black sites' after 9-11 and didn't we torture people in the name of national security? Maybe you're right. Maybe they just haul her back to jail when they're finished with her. Who knows, maybe she is already dead?"

"Now that would be a comforting thought," said Haden.

Chapter Thirty-Four
Saint Petersburg, Russia

Arkady Boromir was in his cubicle working on code for the next Evil Corp hack when the elevator at the far end of the open work space opened and a body fell out. It was Vladimir Tchernoff who stepped out for a coffee some twenty minutes earlier. He was bleeding profusely from the throat. From behind him a woman stepped out of the elevator and the bullets began flying. In his panic Boromir noted she was a blonde dressed in black tights and a white shirt with black polka dots. The snub-nosed submachine gun in her arms was blazing. All around him his co-workers went down with huge holes in their torsos. He could smell cordite and the iron smell of blood in the air around him as he dove for the floor under his desk knocking the little vase of chamomile flowers onto the floor.

He could hear the woman step from desk to desk occasionally firing a short burst, probably to finish someone off. She seemed to be in a hurry. Suddenly, he saw her standing over him. Despite his panic he was struck by her beauty, pale skin, huge blue eyes, long blonde hair. Surely, she must be Russian. "Close your eyes, Mischa, and go to sleep," she said in Russian as she fired a short burst at his head.

Once Ariella finished off every-one she could find on the fifth floor she jumped into the elevator and went up to the sixth. She only had two magazines left. She exited the elevator on the sixth floor firing rapidly. Everyone on the floor ducked for cover. She pulled the pin on the first grenade, tossed it into the elevator and took cover behind a desk. The explosion covered the immediate area with shards of metal and the elevator was permanently disabled buying her a little more time. Any pursuers would have to get through the doors to the stairs and climb six stories. She carefully cleared the room trying to use as few rounds as possible. Fortunately, there were fewer employees up here. Mostly tech people, she guessed. Finally, after passing through two office areas she came to the server room. A row of six servers stood humming with lights blinking. At the far end of the room was a utility closet. There she found what she was looking for. Roof access.

She backed into the utility closet, checked the trap door at the top of the roof access ladder to make sure it would open and tossed all three grenades at the servers, closed the door to the closet and started up the ladder. She could hear the roar of the explosion and the crackle of flames from the fire it started. She did not stop to admire her handiwork or look down at the street to see the reaction to the shooting and explosions. She could hear sirens and they sounded close.

The Vordinsky palace had a mansard roof as did the neighboring building. They were close enough together that she could cross over easily. The next building had a peaked roof and she balanced precariously to get across. The next building was a modern office building with a flat roof terrace and roof access doors. She quickly took off the backpack she was carrying and took out a plain, cotton, gray dress, and a pair of espadrilles. She changed out of her tights and blouse, removed her blonde wig, stuffed the clothes and Uzi into the backpack but kept the wig, stuffing it into a pocket of the dress. She left the backpack under a pile of trash on the corner of the roof and entered the rooftop access.

She found herself in a janitorial closet. She peered out into the adjacent hallway and, seeing no one, stepped out. The first thing she did was look for a public restroom where she flushed the blonde wig down a toilet. The elevator at the end of the corridor took her down to the lobby where a large group of people were gathered at the building entrance and on the street. "What's going on?" she asked.

"We're not sure," someone answered, "but a lot of police and firetrucks are at a building down the block."

Ariella nodded and walked out onto the street. She returned to her hotel on foot, checked out and took a taxi to the Vitebsky railway station. She waited an hour for a train to Pavlovsk.

Chapter Thirty-Five
Bogota, Colombia

They were meeting in a conference room at Carlos Bonilla's club. Mostly there were financial matters to hash out because of increased sales in the New York City area. They also needed to discuss the matter of Bonilla's assassin who somehow disappeared from the American federal prison system.

"Is it possible that someone else has already taken care of this woman?" asked Juna Solis.

"My contacts indicate she may have cut some sort of a deal with the authorities but that it did not involve us. I think you can see that our sales volume has not been impacted by her arrest and in fact that the death of Morales has resulted in more profits," answered Bonilla.

"Do we need to worry about her?" asked Roberto Alfaro.

"Well, it appears that she is either dead or no longer in custody. We can't be sure. Either way I don't see her as a danger to us. She never knew much about the cartel anyway. I do think we will miss her as a useful tool though. Look at all she accomplished while working for us," responded Bonilla.

"Still, she got caught," said Solis.

"There is always risk, we are engaged in a risky business," answered Bonilla. "You've seen colleagues go down in the past. Even someone as great as Escobar lost his life in the end. What we have gotten from this assassin is invaluable, cleaning the streets of competition in Los Angeles, killing Lucero and destabilizing *Los Urbenos*, getting rid of that leech Morales, and even neutralizing a dissenting voice among you in Escalante. I'm not sure how she failed after killing Morales, but it did not end up hurting us."

"You sound a bit defensive, Bonilla," said Zaragosa. "After all you used this killer without even knowing what sex she was. Maybe you took too big a risk hiring her. We still don't know where she is or what she told anyone about us. You say she is not in custody but we have no clue where she is. Maybe she is working for the Feds now?"

"Well, if we hear from her, we can try to take care of her," said Bonilla. "Tracking her down may be difficult. She always made every effort to stay anonymous, which we liked. We have no idea where her base is. It is not going to be like putting a hit on her in prison. Look, right now I am not too worried. The woman has never met any of us, doesn't know our names and knows nothing about our business. All she ever knew was who we wanted her to hit. I think we can move on without a lot of anxiety about her being a danger to us in the future."

Around the table heads nodded, although no one smiled.

Chapter Thirty-Six
Pavlovsk, Russia

The Pavlovsk station was simply a platform with a ticket office and tea stand attached. There was no sign indicating what town the station served. Had she not spoken Russian and understood the announcement over the loudspeaker in her car, Ariella would not have known to get off. She climbed down from the passenger car and walked along the platform wondering if Ospina was going to turn up. She peered out into the car park and saw a tall, blonde woman sitting in a black Kia sedan.

"Congratulations," said Ospina as Ariella opened the door to get in. "You're hit was successful beyond anything we could have hoped. It puts Evil Corp temporarily out of service, deprives them of their best hackers and should be a discouragement to future recruits. Of course, the Kremlin will keep this as quiet as they can but word gets out."

"You didn't think I would get out alive, did you?" asked Ariella.

"Frankly, no," answered Ospina. "It does tend to make things a little more complicated." She backed the car out of its parking place and drove through the little village of white washed wooden cottages. There was a butcher shop and greengrocer in the middle of town but not much else. Within a few minutes they were driving through small vegetable farms with neat patches of cabbage, potatoes and carrots and small, wooden peaked roof farmhouses. After a few miles of that they began passing large fields of waving golden grain, wheat, barley, and corn. There were no houses in sight any longer.

"There's no small airport anywhere near here is there?"

"My dear, Ariella, how perceptive you are," said Ospina as she pulled out a Glock 19M from her purse and pointed it at Ariella. They drove for a few more miles before Ospina pulled over next to a barley field. "Why don't we take a little walk?" she asked motioning with the Glock for her to get out of the car.

Chapter Thirty-Seven
Saint Petersburg, Russia

Detective Vladimir Omsky had never witnessed a scene quite like that at the Pantera offices in the old Vordinsky palace. They had to access the fifth and sixth floor by the stairs since the elevator had been blown up by a grenade. On the fifth-floor bodies lay everywhere. The smell of blood and cordite was still strong in the air, mixed with smoke from the fire on the sixth floor. Omsky worked for the investigative division of the *Politsiya Rossii*, the national police who had been assigned priority to investigate this attack.

The entire building had been evacuated with uniformed police cordoning off the area all around. Firefighters had extinguished the blaze on the sixth floor but the damage was extensive. Omsky counted over forty bodies on the fifth floor alone. Nine-millimeter shells lay scattered over the floor. Ballistics should be able to tell what sort of weapon had been used. A middle-aged man in a dark suit approached him. "Noam Blinsky, FSB," he said flashing a badge. "Tell me what happened here."

"The security guard in the lobby said a blonde woman in black tights and a white blouse with black polka dots wearing a backpack raced after one of the coders who was entering Pantera's private elevator. She dove in and the elevator went on up to the fifth floor. From here we have no eye witnesses for what happened after but we speculate she slit the coder's throat in the elevator and used his pass card to get up to the fifth floor. She exited the elevator with some sort of automatic weapon blazing and took out everyone on the floor. She then went up to the sixth floor and took out everyone up there, tossing a grenade into the elevator behind her to disable it. She then tossed several grenades at the server array which not only destroyed them but started a fire up there. As far as we can tell she must have exited to the roof. We have men scouring the roof and those nearby. We're not sure which way she went."

"Can anyone provide any identifying information for this woman? Did anyone hear her speak?" asked Blinsky.

"As a matter of fact, the lobby security guard heard her call after the coder to hold the elevator. She spoke Russian with a Petersburg accent," answered Omsky.

Blinsky nodded. His first suspicion had been that the Americans would want to disable Pantera. There were groups, however, that opposed Putin. They were especially active in Saint Petersburg. Perhaps this was the work of an opposition group with help from the CIA. In any case Blinsky felt that news of this attack must be suppressed for it would potentially expose the aggressive activity of the Putin regime which had been repeatedly denied. In addition, the success of the attack would make the regime seem weak and vulnerable. He was already formulating a press release blaming the explosion and deaths on a gas leak.

"Look, detective," said Blinsky, "all paperwork on this case is to be forwarded to FSB with no copies retained. No press release is to be made. FSB will handle that. I want your officers advised to keep quiet about what happened here. Do you understand?" Omsky nodded. It was exactly how he expected they would want this incident handled.

Chapter Thirty-Eight
New York City

Elise Bloom frowned as she held her cell phone to her ear. On the other end a federal prison official was explaining that Ariella Blumkin was no longer available for interview sessions.

"I don't understand," she protested "I've had no problem scheduling sessions for her in the past. She is being held at Met pending trial. I haven't finished my evaluation yet and need another session with her."

This was not true. She had everything she needed to evaluate Blumkin's fitness for trial and eventual assignment to a high security prison in the federal system. She simply wanted to see Ariella again. The memory of that kiss when they last parted still lingered on her lips.

"Miss Blumkin's case has been disposed of. She is no longer in custody," said the voice on the other end of the phone, "I can't tell you much more than that. I'm sorry."

"Do you mean to say she has been released?" protested Elise. "She was accused of multiple murders. She is potentially dangerous. I don't understand."

"She is in a program, supervised release. That's all I can say. I assure you she is no danger to anyone right now," said the voice.

"Is there any way I can contact her?"

"Definitely not. Doctor Bloom, why would you want to do that? Since she is out of the prison system, she is no longer your concern. We don't need a report on her now. I don't see us needing one in the foreseeable future. She is no longer your concern."

The line clicked and went dead. Whatever Ariella's status she was beyond Elise's reach now.

Elise was not sure what to think about any of this. Somehow, Ariella had been spirited away by the system. Elise doubted that this was a benefit for Ariella. The woman had killed two FBI agents along with a host of others. No one was going to give someone like that a break. She would be considered disposable, possibly enticed with the possibility of freedom waved in front of her. Ultimately though criminals like Ariella did not get the benefit of special deals. This saddened Elise. There was something about the woman she found attractive, even strangely admirable. She was fearless, beautiful, and confident in a way Elise had never been. She flaunted her beauty, even in prison denims, while Elise always tried to hide hers. There were lessons to be learned from this strange woman, but Elise had not known her long enough or well enough to learn them. Then too, there was that kiss which still burned her lips whenever she thought about it.

Chapter Thirty-Nine
Outside Pavlosk, Russia

They pushed through the rows of golden barley four feet high on either side of them. Ariella walked in front of Ospina who held a gun in her back.

"Well, it was nice getting to know a fellow child of Russian immigrants. It's too bad you were so successful. We hoped you would die in the hit but we always had a contingency ready just in case. I guess we underestimated you. Who knows, if your life had taken a different turn, you would have made a good CIA agent instead of ending up dead in a Russian barley field."

"I thought we had a deal. I do the hit and you let me go so long as I don't go back to the U.S."

"The Agency doesn't do deals. If you believed what you were told then you were a fool. The Agency doesn't want you around as a potential source of information on this plan. What if you went to the press? What if the Russians got hold of you? Besides you were going to get the death sentence anyway. This way your death accomplishes something. Straight ahead," ordered Ospina pushing Ariella with her free hand.

Ariella seemed to stumble, then kicked back with her right leg while simultaneously jerking her right arm back into Ospina's, knocking the gun away from Ariella's back. The kick threw Ospina off balance and Ariella whirled around and punched Ospina hard in the face with a closed fist.

Ospina lunged backward from the force of the blow. She still held the gun. Ariella threw herself at Ospina grabbing her right arm and lifting the gun up. The gun fired into the air and Ariella threw another punch with her right hand knocking Ospina to the ground. Straddling her Ariella grabbed Ospina's gun hand with her left hand and drew her right hand tightly around Ospina's throat. Ospina's left hand flailed at Ariella trying to punch her in the face. Ariella bobbed her head to avoid the full force of the blows and tightened her grip on Ospina's throat. She had done this before with a stronger victim. Within a few minutes Ospina stopped struggling and was no longer breathing. Ariella checked her pulse and confirmed the woman was dead. "You really didn't think it would be so easy, did you?" she said to the corpse

She picked up the gun and rifled through Ospina's purse finding two full magazines for the Glock and Ospina's identification along with sixty-two thousand Russian rubles. There was also the key to the Kia. She stripped the clothes off the dead woman and dragged her naked body deeper into the barley field. With any luck it would not be found until harvest time and, even then, might be ripped to shreds by a thresher. She took Ospina's clothes and purse making her way through the barley back to the road. She climbed into the Kia turning on the GPS on Ospina's phone to get directions back to Saint Petersburg.

She stopped at a roadside café and dropped Ospina's clothes and empty purse in a trash receptacle. Ospina's identification she flushed down a toilet in the café restroom. The drive to Finlyandskiy train station in Saint Petersburg was uneventful. She left the Kia in a car park several blocks from the station and walked. She purchased a first-class ticket to Helsinki and sat in the waiting room for the hour and a half before her train was to leave.

It was late afternoon by the time she settled into her first-class compartment. During her wait she purchased a newspaper and watched the television screen in the waiting area. There was no mention of any violence at Pantera corporation offices. She was not surprised.

The train stopped at Vainikkala, Finland on the Russian Finnish border for passport control. The Finnish immigration officer barely looked at her French passport. From there another two hours and she was in Helsinki. From the train station she took a taxi to Helsinki-Vantaa airport where, after ditching the Glock in a restroom trash can, she was able to book a midnight flight to Paris. After a night in a hotel and a good meal in a brasserie, she caught the Air France flight to Guadeloupe.

Chapter Forty
New York City

Haden's favorite lunch place was Bruno's. It was a few blocks away from her office and known for having good hamburgers. It was not exactly Marcie Quinn's sort of place but she still rode the subway from the Federal Building to meet Haden there. Haden was sitting in a booth looking at a menu as Quinn entered. As usual she was carefully dressed in a tight, blue wool skirt with a cream-colored sleeveless linen blouse. Unlike Haden, Quinn often went out without her sidearm. "It's bulky and it ruins the look of my outfit," she told Haden.

Over the past few months Quinn had become the best friend Haden ever had. They spent most week-ends together and often met for lunch. Despite their many differences Haden never felt more comfortable or accepted by someone. She felt she could say anything to Quinn. The woman's dry sense of humor often made Haden laugh. As she made her way through the restaurant to the booth Haden noticed how tight the little skirt was over Quinn's pert little ass. *Why am I looking at another woman's ass?* thought Haden.

"Hey girl," said Quinn as she sat down.

She was a short, slightly built girl with short blonde hair and big blue eyes. She wore lots of make-up. As she sat down Haden noted her bare, shapely legs as she crossed them. She was wearing red patent leather four-inch heels.

"You're late," said Haden smiling. She found herself always happy to see Quinn. "I was just about to order. I have to get back soon. I have a ton of paperwork sitting on my desk."

"So, let's eat," responded Quinn. "Anything exciting happening in your shop?"

"It seems the death of Morales hasn't slowed down the Medellin cartel. They've gone after a few of the guys who worked for him. Drive by stuff, nothing as ballsy as what the Ariella girl did. I bet they miss her."

"Frankly, I'm surprised they didn't take her out once she was arrested. I guess, though, from what I have heard she spent her time mostly in solitary. Hard to get to her there," answered Quinn.

"How about you, Marcie. Anything interesting happening at the FBI?"

"No, they have me working white collar crime. So dull, all about numbers and stock trades. It was more fun tracking killers with you."

The fact that Quinn was now working white collar crime signaled to Haden that Quinn had moved up in the FBI hierarchy. Despite her ultrafeminine style and Barbie looks, the woman was smart and perceptive. Haden suspected that people were always underestimating her. They ordered. Haden getting a cheeseburger with French fries and Quinn opting for a cobb salad.

"Your place or mine this week-end?" asked Quinn.

"Obviously mine," answered Haden as she did every time Quinn asked the question.

Haden had a relatively spacious one-bedroom apartment in Queens while Quinn rented a tiny studio in midtown Manhattan. "You know I'm claustrophobic."

Quinn smiled and put her hand briefly on Haden's. although the touch was brief Haden felt her pulse race and her heart flutter.

Chapter Forty-One
CIA Headquarters, Langley, Virginia.

The conference room lacked windows and was lit by aging fluorescent fixtures. The group sitting around the table, each nursing a paper cup of CIA coffee, was almost the same as had met three months earlier to discuss the Russian hacking problem. Mark Fulham, CIA assistant director, Marcie Bernard CIA Russia desk chief and special agent Cecily Gleeson. Missing from the earlier meeting was State Department Russia desk chief Gene Falk and special agent Nadia Ospina. It was Ospina's absence that prompted the meeting. "What's the latest word on Ospina?" asked Fulham.

"She hasn't been seen or heard from since the day of the hit," said Bernard. "We've traced her movements up to that day. She flew into Moscow a few days ahead of the hit and went from there to Saint Petersburg. She arranged for the delivery of the weapon to Blumkin with the Israeli consulate there. On the day of the hit, she was at the Hermitage Museum when Blumkin started shooting. On her arrival at Saint Petersburg, she rented a Kia sedan. When she heard the sirens on the street responding to the attack, she drove her Kia to the train station at Pavlovsk, a small, rural suburb where she arranged to meet Blumkin if she survived. Of course, she had no idea whether or not Blumkin actually survived. She planned to wait at the station until the last train from Saint Petersburg arrived. Like the rest of us she doubted Blumkin would get away."

"But she did," said Gleeson.

"As far as we know she did," continued Bernard, "but the Russians have hushed this entire event up so we don't know too much. Inside sources have told us that the hacker group got hit very hard and are out of circulation for a while, maybe forever. We've had no word that anyone was captured or killed but we can't be sure. The rented Kia was recently found by the rental agency in a car park in central Saint

Petersburg. No trace of Ospina and we haven't heard from her since the day of the hit and it has now been over a month."

"Do we assume she's dead?" asked Gleeson.

"I don't think we can assume anything," said Fulham.

"As far as we know she did her job then disappeared. There might be a lot of different explanations for that. One of which is that she is dead. I can't imagine FSB would be so bold as to take her out. She was at pains to be seen at the Hermitage Museum while the action went down at Pantera."

"She was a known CIA agent, though," said Bernard. "That's why she had to be transferred out of the Moscow embassy. We have to assume FSB was keeping an eye on her."

"That's why she was at the museum when the shooting happened. It's not likely she would have driven to Pavlovsk if she thought she was being followed. I think the hit took all of FSB's resources so she was free to get away," said Gleeson." Is it possible the Blumkin woman took her out before Ospina could take her down?"

"If that's the case," said Bernard "then why is there no trace of Blumkin? We are pretty sure she didn't fly out of Saint Petersburg since we were monitoring the airport. Is it possible Ospina flipped? Her parents were Russian."

"Ospina hated the regime," responded Gleeson. "I can't imagine her ever going over."

"All of this is just speculation," said Fulham. "We have no idea what might have happened. If FSB did take Ospina out, and I doubt they did, they will let us know in some way just to send a message. If Blumkin got away she'll show up eventually somewhere. If we can't find her, the Russians won't be able to find her either, so maybe our secrets are safe."

"Still, she would be a loose end if she ever did turn up. She could always go to the press," added Bernard.

"She doesn't strike me as the type who deals with the press," responded Fulham. "Besides she is still on the hook for eleven murders if she sets foot on American soil. I doubt she would want any publicity assuming she is even alive."

Chapter Forty-Two
Villa Dupleve, Guadeloupe, French Caribbean

Ariella awakened to grey skies and a strong, warm wind sweeping off the Caribbean. These were the periphery of hurricane Zelda which was calculated to just miss the island which hit Puerto Rico and was heading towards Grenada. The air, usually lightened by cool breezes from the sea, felt heavy and oppressive. Ariella found herself weighted by something she never before felt, depression.

She wondered if this strange feeling was the result of post-traumatic stress. After all she had been arrested, spent months in solitary confinement in prison, been threatened with the death penalty only to be released to undertake a suicidal attack in a hostile country, then face an assassination attempt by her own country.

There would be no swimming today as the ocean was turbulent and heavy rain was likely so there would be no lounging in the sun with a bottle of champagne. She had been home for three months now since her escape from Saint Petersburg. As far as she could tell there had been no fall-out, at least as far as she was concerned, from her attack on the nest of hackers in Saint Petersburg. There was no mention in the news of any mass killing in Russia. Obviously, the Kremlin hushed it up. The U.S. government, the message having been sent, had no desire to associate itself with the mayhem. Ariella did a public service for her country. She was under no illusion that she was some sort of hero. She did it to obtain her release from prison, not to stop the ransomware hacking. She was fully aware that when the deed was done, they would try to eliminate her. It was a chance she was willing to take. Now she was free but with a sense of ennui she had not previously experienced. Perhaps the answer to that would be a talented therapist.

Before she could think too much about the future there was something she needed to do. She was ready for change, for finding a new way to live taking fewer chances and enjoying life more. She had enough money. She had most of the things she wanted in life. If she stopped killing for money it was not because of morality, her only morality was her own need. It was in search of tranquility. Neither anger nor rage drove her to kill. Instead, it was a kind of savagery that drove her. That savagery was lately winding down to be replaced with a sense of emptiness and restlessness.

All her life those close to her considered her emotionally disfigured. She did things that horrified most people. By the moral standards of society, she was, as her late mother and first real lover opined, a monster. It was not even what she did but her lack of remorse, the utter absence of guilt, which bothered others. She remembered the look of her late boyfriend's face when she slit the throat of a University of Chicago coed right in front of him. The horror reflected on that face let her know the relationship could not be sustained. At least so long as she led a lifestyle of murder and mayhem there were few, if any, who would share her life.

For her, the question was, did her present ennui reflect a change? If she no longer felt the drive of her inner savagery, did this mean she could lead a different kind of life? The prison therapist, Elise, classified her as a psychopath. Was this a condition for which there could be a cure? Did she even want to be cured? Was there a benefit to suddenly being open to emotions like guilt, remorse, envy, even love?

Chapter Forty-Three
New York City

Autumn in New York could be a very melancholy time. As the skies became more often gray, the leaves began to change and the days became shorter it was hard not to think about the passage of time and the passing of things. To many people autumn could be a time of excitement. There was a new Broadway season, people returning to the city from their summer retreats, a new social season with parties and concerts. None of these things mattered to Elise. She hated Broadway shows from the time she was a child and the family always had tickets to the latest hit. The music and stories seemed simplistic and insipid. These days, as someone who studied human behavior for a living, she simply found the shows irrelevant. She no longer went to parties. She found her circle of friends dwindling especially as her female friends married and started families. As for male friends, well, how could you really be friends with a man?

Her practice was thriving. Her reputation as a therapist was impeccable. She was considering not renewing her contract with the Federal Bureau of Prisons as she could make more money devoting the time to her private practice. It was true that some of her prison patients were far more interesting than anyone in her private practice. The only problem was that her exposure to them was minimal. She could only see a prison patient two or three times at the most. The extent of her work with them was limited to fitness for trial and assignment to the appropriate level of prison facility. There was no chance to delve into the factors that drove the more severely depraved prisoners to commit their crimes. The psychopaths seemed like almost another species of human with an alternate set of emotions or lack thereof. She wondered if there might be possibilities to engage in research that could be more fulfilling than the sort of clinical therapy in which she was currently engaged.

New York itself was weighing on her. It seemed increasingly to be a crowded, noisy, dirty city full of rude or indifferent people. Once she gloried in the city, it's museums, concerts, restaurants, and galleries. Increasingly she found it too burdensome to take advantage of the things the city offered. After a long day of soaking up other people's emotional chaos she often just settled into her sofa with a glass of wine and listened to music or lay in bed watching documentaries on PBS. Her love life withered to nothing. Her friends were often too busy with children and family to have time to socialize as they had in the past.

She wasn't old, just barely thirty. Her perception of life was beginning to change and it made her feel older than her years. Perhaps it was time to take a year off and travel. Time to look for new experiences and take a fresh look at everything. She sighed. She knew herself well enough that she almost certainly lacked the courage to try something like that.

Chapter Forty-Four
Queens, New York

Ariella was surprised. The lock on the apartment door was easy to pick and the deadbolt had been left unlocked. It was a second-floor unit and she got one of the other tenants to buzz her in. The living room, empty now at three in the morning, had a stark, unlived in quality. There was a small sofa, a glass coffee table, two barstools at the peninsula which separated the living room from the kitchen which undoubtedly served as a dining counter. On the wall was a Toulouse Lautrec print of the Moulin Rouge. A fake oriental rug lay on the manufactured wood floor.

She pulled out her Beretta and screwed on the silencer before entering the hallway. On one side was a full bathroom with a very messy counter full of cosmetics and hair products. On the other side of the hallway a door was slightly ajar. Ariella slid into the room as quietly as a cat. It was a small bedroom with a queen-sized bed. In the bed curled up together were two naked women, Becky Haden, and Marcie Quinn. Ariella smiled to herself. It had been Haden she wanted to find; the smart, tough detective who had been clever enough to track her down and arrest her. Quinn had been in on the arrest as well so finding her was an added bonus.

The last time she encountered Haden before the arrest she was pregnant by the nerdy fool FBI agent who had been her temporary partner. Ariella felt she was doing Haden a favor by taking the man's forehead off with a shot from an AR15. Since there was no sign of a child in the apartment Haden had either aborted or given it up for adoption. On reflection Ariella was not too surprised that Haden's affair with that FBI agent put her off men. She could see the attraction of Quinn; cute, feminine with enough moxie to qualify as an FBI agent and even get assigned to tracking down Ariella Blumkin. They made a cute couple.

Seeing them made Ariella think. Somehow these two law

enforcement types, each very different from the other, found each other. Were Ariella to refrain from killing them perhaps they would live happily ever after. Why couldn't she find the same sort of happiness?

"Becky, darling, this is your wakeup call sweetie," Ariella called out.

Haden disengaged herself from Quinn, rolled over and looked up.

"You're dead," she said half asleep.

"Not quite, dear. Like a cockroach I'm just not that easy to kill."

Quinn stirred but did not wake. Ariella aimed her gun at Haden, who was now sitting up in bed staring at her goggle eyed. The shot hit her in the middle of the forehead waking Quinn.

"Sorry to invade your little love nest dear but after all I do have a score to settle, don't I?"

The second shot got Quinn in the neck as she twisted away to try to avoid it. Ariella stepped toward the bed and shot her in the forehead, just to be sure. "I'm sorry I didn't say it earlier when you were both still alive but you two make a darling couple, really you do."

Chapter Forty-Five
New York City

Elise was in her apartment sipping wine and reading a recently published paper "Emotion Regulation Therapy for Generalized Anxiety Disorder with and Without Co-Occurring Depression." It was certainly relevant to her practice as her patients increasingly reported higher levels of anxiety to the point where they were feeling physical symptoms. As she got up to refill her wine glass her cell phone rang. She was not expecting a call and she did not recognize the caller's number. Curious as to who it might be at this time in the evening she answered.

"Doctor Bloom?" said a vaguely familiar voice on the other end of the line.

"Yes, who is this please?"

"It's Ariella Blumkin. Formerly an inmate at the Metropolitan Correctional Center and formerly a patient of yours, sort of."

Elise went numb.

"Of course, I remember you Ariella. Are you back in prison? I got the impression from the prison authorities that you had been released under some sort of special arrangement."

"True enough. I'm a free woman now. I did a favor for the authorities and they let me go." Ariella's voice sounded amused.

"They let you go? You were accused of murdering eleven people including an FBI agent. They don't let people like that go."

"Well, they did me. I'm special, but you already know that, don't you Doctor Bloom?"

"Yes, Ariella, you are unique. There is no doubt about that. Why are you calling me? How did you get my cell number?"

"How I got your cell number is a trade secret. I'm very good at researching information; it's a trait that has probably saved my life more than once. I'm calling you, Elise, to invite you to come visit me."

"What? I don't understand."

"Take some time off and come visit me. I'll send you a plane ticket. I have a beautiful home in a tropical paradise, my own private beach and lots of bananas. Come stay for a while. We can get to know each other better. I found myself liking you a lot. So, I'd like to spend some time with you. It could be a very pleasant vacation for you."

Elise swallowed hard. She could not believe what she was hearing. It was even harder for her to believe how close she was to saying "yes."

"Look, Ariella, I don't mean to be blunt but you are a psychopathic murderer. How comfortable do you think I would feel stepping into your lair so to speak?"

"I know. My own mother called me a monster. My first boyfriend called me a monster and my last boyfriend tried to leave me because he was appalled at what he saw me do. I have done terrible things and, to be honest, it never really occurred to me that they were terrible. I've gone through a lot in the last few months and I understand that my life needs to change. I want to change. Part of my changing involves getting to know you better, Elise. You have my word that I would never hurt you and that I would never involve you in something that would compromise your conscience."

"I don't know what to say," responded Elise.

"Just say 'yes.' Come for as short or as long a time as you want. I'm not worried about you revealing anything about me because where I am I cannot be extradited."

"Where are you exactly?"

"A beautiful island in the Caribbean. The food is wonderful, the trade winds blow off my back door. You'll like it."

"Can I think about it for a bit?"

"Of course. We have the rest of our lives. Let's not waste too much time. Why don't I contact you in two weeks? Is that enough time?"

"I guess so. I have to say I'm very confused by all this."

"Me too. Bye, Elise. Talk to you in two weeks.

Chapter Forty-Six
Queens, New York

Detective Ermina Gonzales was badly shaken. The first reason was that her boss, Detective Becky Haden, had been found in her bed shot through the head. The second reason was that she had been found stark naked in bed with an equally naked female FBI agent. Gonzales had no clue that her boss and partner, a woman she looked up to, respected deeply, was a lesbian. Gonzales came from an old school Catholic, Puerto Rican family. Being gay was not accepted. Now Gonzales was finding out that her friend and partner was gay. Of course, the murder was a bigger deal but not by much.

The FBI agent had also been shot. She had been hit twice, in the neck and forehead. Gonzales knew her. She worked with Haden on a bust of some female professional killer. They subsequently became best friends after the agent, Marcie Quinn, was assigned to the New York Bureau office. Haden was always going to lunch with her and hanging out with her when they were both off duty. Neither one of them was exactly 'butch.' Haden was an attractive woman who had, in the past, dated men. Quinn was an ultra-feminine type who wore tight skirts, lots of jewelry, make-up and short, frosted hair. The guys in homicide were always ogling her whenever she was around. She didn't look like a lesbian or FBI agent.

The sheets on the bed were covered with blood. Gonzales hoped the medical examiners would finish soon so the bodies could be covered and taken away. There were already a couple of FBI agents on-scene. Forensics could find no fingerprints, no brass, no evidence of any kind. The front door to Haden's apartment had been picked but everything else in the apartment seemed to have been left alone. The killer apparently picked the front door lock, went straight to the bedroom, and shot the two women just as they were stirring from sleep. He probably left the way he came in.

Gonzales worked a lot of cases with Haden. Most of the people they arrested were still in jail. She could not think of who might have enough of a grudge against her to shoot her. Perhaps Haden's love life might render some clues about a possible killer. Jealousy was always a strong motive.

A middle-aged woman with graying blonde hair in a pony-tail wearing a gray flannel pants suit walked into the room. She flashed an FBI badge. "I'm Assistant Director Patricia Patterson," she said to Gonzales. "Are you the investigating officer?"

"I guess so," said Gonzales, "at least for now. Becky Haden was my partner and supervisor, so I guess I'm involved no matter what."

"I knew Detective Haden," said Patterson. "She was involved in several investigations with the Bureau. They all had to do with the same killer, a woman. Haden was an excellent officer. I happened to be in town from D.C. for a series of meetings and when I heard that Quinn went down, I rushed over. I didn't realize she was involved with Haden. I wouldn't have expected that of either one of them."

"That woman killer," asked Gonzales, "could she have done this?"

"It's possible I guess," said Patterson. "No one seems to have any idea where she is, not even the CIA."

"CIA?" interrupted Gonzales. "What do they have to do with this?"

"Their involvement is above your pay grade, detective. For that matter it's above mine as well. All I know now is that the CIA somehow broke her loose against the strong objection of the Bureau. Now they seem to have lost her, perhaps disposed of her and are unwilling to admit it. So, the short answer to your question is I simply don't know if that woman had anything to do with this or even if she is still alive. You know the CIA are very good at cleaning up loose ends."

Gonzales eyed the bodies on the blood-soaked bed. The medical examiners were just about to wind up their examination and attendants wheeled in two gurneys to remove the bodies. As they slipped body bags over the two naked bodies, Gonzales felt a tear roll down her cheek. Haden had been smart, tough, fair and a wonderful mentor. Suddenly, Gonzales felt very alone.

Chapter Forty-Seven
Pointe-A-Pitre, Guadeloupe, French Caribbean

Elise peered out the plane porthole as it skimmed over the roofline of a small city then passed over green fields. The runway was surrounded by trees as the plane taxied to the single modern terminal. Her palms were sweaty as she gathered her carry-on items to deplane. This trip may have been a huge mistake. She had no idea what she was getting herself into. Psychopaths are dangerous. They did not suddenly cure themselves or turn into normal, caring human beings. Ariella Blumkin was clearly a psychopath and had proven herself to be a dangerous one. Only a fool would rush to meet someone like that. She was definitely a fool.

She had no problem getting through immigration. Guadeloupe was a French island so her United States passport was readily accepted and she needed no special visa. As she walked out the arriving passengers' exit, she saw her. Ariella was dressed in tight fitting, faded blue jeans with a sleeveless, V-necked cotton blouse. Her long, black hair shimmered. For a woman living in the tropics her skin was surprisingly pale. Around her neck on a silver chain was a pale blue sapphire that matched her eyes. When she saw Elise she stepped toward her, put her arms around her and kissed her. Elise was stunned but waves of pleasure surged though her body.

"Well, I'm here," she managed to gasp.

"I can see that," said Ariella with a faint smile, "and I'm glad you are."

She took Elise's bag and walked her to the car park where she unlocked an old Land Rover and loaded the bag. The air was warm but a strong, cool breeze blew off the ocean. There was a faint floral smell in the air. The Land Rover wound its way through narrow streets lined with buildings that were a mix of French colonial, with columns, arches, and European modern with clean, bland lines. Everyone on the streets was

Black.

"I have a villa on Basse-Terre, the western half of the island. It's just west of a city called Goyave. It's about an hour and a half drive so I thought maybe we could stop in Goyave for lunch."

"That sounds great," she hesitated. "Look, to be entirely honest I'm not sure what I'm doing here. I'm not even sure what you are doing here. The last time we met you were in a prison jump suit and I was evaluating whether or not you should go to a high security federal prison. Now suddenly, you are dressed in resort clothes, living in a villa on a tropical island in the Caribbean. Somehow you disappeared from the prison system altogether. I am drawn to you. I admit you are beautiful, smart and confident like no one else I have ever met. You were in prison for a reason, a very good reason. I have to admit I'm afraid of you."

Ariella smiled as she piloted the Land Rover out of Point-A-Pitre onto the coastal highway. The water glistened deep blue under a pale blue, cloudless sky. The shore was lined with coconut palms. Here and there Elise caught a glimpse of slivers of pristine white beach. As they moved out of the city the landscape became thick forest on either side of the road.

"It's beautiful, isn't it?" said Ariella. "The weather will hold until this evening when it will probably rain but we should enjoy a lovely day. Look, I understand how you feel. My own mother called me a 'monster.' So did my first boyfriend. I can't say they were wrong. There is more to me than that. I liked you the moment I first saw you, Elise. I would never hurt you under any circumstances. There was a guy in my life a while back. A guy named Fred. We had fun together watching movies, listening to music, traveling. Fred didn't know me and when he saw the monster side of me, he panicked. He couldn't accept me for what I was. You know the worst about me, Elise. You know what I've done. Yet you're still here. That means a lot."

They rode silently for a while occasionally passing though little towns made up of brightly painted cement block cottages with corrugated metal roofs. Occasionally they passed a banana grove or a field of pineapple.

Goyave was a larger town filled with brightly painted wooden buildings. Ariella pulled up close to a white clapboard structure with orange shutters and a sign that read in script 'La Conque.' The restaurant was half empty when they went in and Ariella headed straight to an empty table. The waiter, a light skinned black man in a white shirt, khaki pants, and a dark blue apron, greeted her effusively in French. The menus he brought them were also in French, a language Elise did not know, with no corresponding English translation.

"What do you like?" asked Ariella. "I can help you order."

Elise ended up with conch fritters, filet of dorado with hollandaise and capers, a green salad and chocolate mousse. It was a meal comparable to the best restaurant in Manhattan. Somehow, they managed to empty a bottle of sauvignon blanc between the two of them. Ariella showed no sign of being affected by the lion's share of wine she consumed.

The road outside Goyave ran through tropical forest with an occasional farm. About twenty minutes outside of Goyave Ariella turned off on a dirt road that ran through groves of bananas. They came to an open gate leading to a crescent shaped flagstone driveway. Ariella pulled up in front of a large pink, stucco French colonial villa with white shutters, arched windows and doors. On the second floor a white wooden balcony ran the length of the house. Ariella unlocked the large arched front door and walked them in to a spacious parlor with a travertine floor. In contrast to the style of the house the furniture was stark, elegant, mid-century modern with a sofa, glass coffee table and end tables. A flight of mahogany stairs led up to the second floor. A large opening led toward the back of the house to an even larger room with a mahogany bar in one corner and a series of glass paned French doors leading out onto an expansive patio. Beyond the patio were stone steps leading to a private beach. In a corner of the room a large stereo with horn speakers and tube amplifiers sat flanked by a mahogany cabinet filled with vinyl records.

Ariella dropped Elise's bag, stepped toward her, and embraced her. Their kiss was long and involved tongues. When Ariella finally released her Elise was weak at the knees. She felt like she was about to faint.

"You'll have your own bedroom but you are welcome at any time to come to mine. I won't pressure you. Stay for as long or as short as you like. But I want you here. Regardless of what you do I will not be living the way I used to live. I may not regret what I've done but I no longer want to take chances. I want to savor life. I want to enjoy everything there is to give pleasure. I'm tired of being alone. I want something more."

"I guess the fact that I've come says something. I have a lot of doubts Ariella, to be honest. There's a lot about you I don't know. I won't judge you, there's no point. You thrill me but you also frighten me. You talk about changing your life. Well, mine seems to be changing too and that's frightening as well. I'm here. I do want to be here. That's about all I can promise."

"That will have to be good enough, at least for now. I can make no promises either but I'm glad you're here."

Ariella took her hand and walked her though the French doors onto the terrace. The sun shone brightly and the dark blue water gleamed with its reflection. The bougainvillea in planters lining the stairs to the beach bristled with reds and purples. A quiet breeze blew off the water.

Also by the Author
at
Rogue Phoenix Press

Curse of Ciudad Blanca

Peter VanOwen is living by the beach in Costa Rica when his old college roommate, a disgraced professor of archaeology, drops in unexpectedly to convince him to go on an expedition to discover a lost city in the Honduran jungle and help resurrect his career. He is enticed to join the expedition by the prospect of seeing once again his long-lost college girlfriend who has remained the love of his life. But once in Honduras he encounters a sinister and mysterious woman who entraps him into going on an expedition he had intended to avoid. Upon penetrating deep into the Honduran jungle in search of the lost city VanOwen comes face to face with a sinister reality that will change his life and that of his family, friends and even his ex-girlfriend.

One
PLAYA ESTERILLOS, COSTA RICA

The rainy season always made his joints ache. Almost every afternoon the clouds gathered over Playa Esterillos, slowly darkening until the sky exploded with thunder, lightning and rain often lasting all night. Peter loved the pounding rain on the tin roof of his roasting shed and the acrid smell of roasting coffee over the humid air.

When he was not visiting coffee growers in the central highlands, he followed the same routine each day. In the warm, dry mornings he stepped out of his compound onto the empty, grey sand beach. He would bring a thermal pot of coffee and lie on his chaise longue reading from his Kindle. Occasionally he entered the warm, calm water. By eleven AM he left the beach to fix a light lunch and check his computer for e-mails. In the afternoon as the humidity rose and the clouds gathered, he would retreat to his roasting shed to sample and experiment with the coffee beans he was considering recommending to his clients in the U.S.

The current batch of beans was from the area around San Vito, a town settled in the nineteen-fifties by Italian immigrants in the southern mountains of central Costa Rica. The beans were plump with promise: smooth and blue-green. His challenge was to find the ideal roast by roasting small batches to various levels, experimenting with temperature and duration. In his shed, he had a small one-kilo Diedrich sample roaster powered by propane. Peter spent his afternoons in the shed roasting batch after batch, sampling the results and recording his findings. He loved the smell, texture and sound of the beans as they progressed through the roasting process.

For Peter, coffee roasting was an escape. Immersion in the process let him lose himself in something outside himself. The deep calm he felt as he processed each batch was the result of escaping his own consciousness and savoring the details of the roast. When the results were good, when he had extracted the ideal balance between body and flavor for the particular bean, he felt a deep sense of satisfaction and accomplishment unconnected with the objective importance of well roasted coffee.

In an earlier life, Peter VanOwen had been a lawyer employed by the Los Angeles County Counsel's office. For a while he had a wife and children and a small house in a Los Angeles suburb. A rancorous divorce and early retirement led him to Costa Rica and a stucco house in a gated compound on the grey volcanic beach of Playa Esterillos on the Pacific coast. He had stumbled into coffee brokering more as a way to fill his days than a need to make money. But he had come to love the process and discovered in himself an entrepreneurial side which had lain dormant over his years as a public lawyer. He bought coffee from small growers and sold it to several modest-sized coffee shop chains in the United States with recommendations on the roast and brewing. He often travelled throughout the central Costa Rican highlands looking for beans and occasionally travelled to Guatemala and Panama. Several times a month he would drive to San José to meet buyers. In between trips, he settled into his comfortable daily routine, seldom communicating with any of his old family and friends in California. His simple, isolated life suited him and he rarely felt a moment of loneliness. He loved the tropical weather, green, lush foliage and the easy, unhurried pace of Costa Rica.

Playa Esterillos had its share of American émigrés but Peter avoided them, as well as the nearby surfer town of Jaco with its high-rise hotels, surf shops and fish taco joints. He drank at home, not wanting to engage in the banal and self-promoting conversation of the typical American bar in Costa Rica. At 60 he had, he admitted to himself, become withdrawn and introspective.

As he watched the temperature on the Diedrich, Peter heard a car pull into his drive. He walked to the shed window to see a hired van expel a slight man with dark rimmed-glasses and ginger-colored hair, a man whom Peter had not seen for many years.

Other Books by the Author
at
Rogue Phoenix Press

Black Orchid
Flowers of Evil Book One

FBI Agent Chandler Diaz was assigned to investigate a string of well executed and brutal homicides in places as far flung as Singapore, Honduras and New York City. Even an investigator as talented as Diaz is having problems solving these crimes. Meanwhile, in Los Angeles, young lawyer, Fred Cornwall, notoriously unsuccessful with the opposite sex, thought he met the girl of his dreams in a kitschy Chinatown bar. She is smart, beautiful and has a lot of secrets. She wines and dines him and dazzles him with her beauty and wealth. But when he starts to learn some of her secrets, and a secret about himself, the dream starts to unravel.

Banana Flower
Flowers of Evil Book Two

In *Black Orchid* the beautiful sociopathic Ariella cut a swath of murders from Singapore to New York City ending with the murder of a senior FBI agent in a New York City hotel room. *Banana Flower* takes up the narrative with the FBI determined to track down the killer and calling prickly but talented former agent Eric VanDerlies out of retirement to lead the effort. He teams in an uneasy partnership with New York homicide detective Becky Haden. The two chase down their killer from Panama to Los Angeles and finally to a confrontation in Costa Rica. Ariella in the meantime has acquired a mansion on the French island of Guadeloupe, changed her alter ego identities and started doing work for a vicious Colombian drug cartel. As in "Black Orchid" her journey leaves a wake of corpses dispatched in a brutal but professional manner. With VanDerlies and Haden hot on her track will her murderous career finally be brought to an end?

The Other Side of Paradise

Aaron Jenks left his surgical practice in Los Angeles along with his wife and two daughters after a nasty divorce to retire to Costa Rica. A chance encounter in a posh Escazu café leads Aaron to the beautiful Nicole L'Heureaux, wife of the head of an old and prominent family whose history parallels the darkest aspects of the history of the Central American nation. Nicole is bored, ambitious and ruthless, unhappy in her marriage and contemptuous of her husband and his family. .Aaron's passion for Nicole leads him to radically change his life and the lives of his daughter and girlfriend in unexpected ways. For Aaron his pursuit of Nicole leads down a dark and desperate path. Costa Rica is a place of great natural beauty but where human passion and greed are involved there is another side to paradise.

About the Author

Robert V Wadden Jr. is a retired attorney splitting his time between his homes in the Los Angeles area and Esterillos, Costa Rica.

www.ingramcontent.com/pod-product-compliance
Lightning Source LLC
Chambersburg PA
CBHW070627130626
46555CB00006B/2472